Girl Detective: A Friday Barnes Mystery
Under Suspicion: A Friday Barnes Mystery
The Adventures of Nanny Piggins
Nanny Piggins and the Wicked Plan
Nanny Piggins and the Runaway Lion
Nanny Piggins and the Accidental Blast-Off
Nanny Piggins and the Rival Ringmaster
Nanny Piggins and the Pursuit of Justice
Nanny Piggins and the Daring Rescue
Nanny Piggins and the Race to Power
The Nanny Piggins Guide to Conquering Christmas

A Friday Barnes Mystery
BIG TROUBLE

R. A. Spratt
Illustrated by Phil Gosier

Roaring Brook Press New York

To Violet and Samantha

Text copyright © 2015 by R. A. Spratt
Illustrations copyright © 2017 by Phil Gosier
Published by Roaring Brook Press
Roaring Brook Press is a division of
Holtzbrinck Publishing Holdings Limited Partnership
175 Fifth Avenue, New York, New York 10010
mackids.com

First published in Australia in 2015 by Penguin Random House Australia

Library of Congress Cataloging-in-Publication Data

Names: Spratt, R. A., author. | Gosier, Phil, 1971–   illustrator.
Title: Big Trouble : A Friday Barnes Mystery / R. A. Spratt ; illustrated by Phil Gosier.
Description: First U.S. edition. | New York : Roaring Brook Press, 2017. |
Series: Friday Barnes mysteries ; [3] | "First published in Australia in 2015 by
Penguin Random House Australia"—Copyright page. | Summary: At her exclusive
boarding school, can super sleuth and girl genius Friday Barnes crack the case of
her missing mother, rein in a royal brat, and unmask the elusive master thief
called the Pimpernel?
Identifiers: LCCN 2016025020 (print) | LCCN 2016048940 (ebook) |
ISBN 9781626726376 (hardcover) | ISBN 9781626726383 (Ebook)
Subjects: | CYAC: Boarding schools—Fiction. | Schools—Fiction. | Genius—Fiction. |
Mystery and detective stories. | BISAC: JUVENILE FICTION / Mysteries &
Detective Stories. | JUVENILE FICTION / Action & Adventure / General. |
JUVENILE FICTION / Girls & Women.
Classification: LCC PZ7.S76826 Fre 2017 (print) | LCC PZ7.S76826 (ebook) |
DDC [Fic]—dc23
LC record available at https://lccn.loc.gov/2016025020

Our books may be purchased in bulk for promotional, educational,
or business use. Please contact your local bookseller or the Macmillan
Corporate and Premium Sales Department at (800) 221-7945 ext. 5442 or
by e-mail at MacmillanSpecialMarkets@macmillan.com.

First U.S. edition 2017
Book design by Anne Diebel
Printed in the United States of America by LSC Communications US,
LLC (Lakeside Classic), Harrisonburg, Virginia

1 3 5 7 9 10 8 6 4 2

Previously in Friday Barnes . . .

In the beginning, Friday Barnes arrived at Highcrest Academy after winning a $50,000 reward for solving a mysterious diamond robbery. She used the money to pay her own tuition fees, believing that at the exclusive boarding school she could relax and enjoy her education. That was before she discovered that Highcrest's wealthy and eccentric students desperately needed help. Because cheating, smuggling, fraud, and all sorts of other mischief were rife at the school. Friday couldn't resist a mystery, so she set herself up as a private detective and was soon finding lost homework, clearing the falsely accused, and solving problems for the Headmaster—including why there was a yeti roaming *around the school swamp, why people kept falling in knee-deep holes, and who the mysterious vagrant living in a van in the forest was. She even uncovered an escaped prisoner enrolled in the school! This book begins just after Friday has received some horrifying news—her father, a world-renowned physicist, has arrived on campus and taken over a science lesson . . .*

The Disappearing Doctor

Friday Barnes was running as fast as she could across the Highcrest Academy campus, which admittedly wasn't too fast because running wasn't her strong suit. She had just heard the shocking news that her father had turned up and taken over a physics lesson, and she was desperate to get to that classroom to minimize whatever public embarrassment he was undoubtedly causing.

Friday's best friend, Melanie Pelly, ran with her, and Ian Wainscott came along as well.

Ian was either Friday's arch nemesis or her love interest. Nobody was quite sure which, least of all Ian and Friday. They were inexplicably drawn to each other, but Friday had put Ian's dad in jail for insurance fraud and it is hard to get past that sort of thing in a relationship. And yet wherever there was a dramatic public confrontation involving Friday, Ian was always there.

When they burst through the classroom door they saw the science teacher, Mr. Davies, slumped at a desk, holding his head in his hands. All the students looked very brain-addled and confused. At the front of the room Friday's father, Dr. Barnes, was scrawling equations over every last square inch of the whiteboard.

"You see here, X is a photon or Z-boson, and here X and Y are two electroweak bosons such that the charge is conserved . . ." droned Dr. Barnes. He had whiteboard marker and egg stains on his saggy brown cardigan, and it didn't look like his hair had been brushed at any time in the last decade.

"Dad, stop!" cried Friday. "You're hurting their brains!"

Dr. Barnes looked up and adjusted his glasses.

"Ah, Friday. Yes, that's why I'm here. I've come to see you."

"Then why have you taken over Mr. Davies's class?" asked Friday.

"I was looking for you when I walked past here," said Dr. Barnes, "and I saw the lesson he was teaching. He clearly needed help. His explanation was childlike."

"These are children," said Friday. "He was explaining physics to children."

Dr. Barnes turned and looked at the class. He adjusted his glasses on his nose again. "Oh yes, I suppose so. I hadn't considered that."

"The family resemblance is remarkable," said Melanie.

"Yes," agreed Ian. "And it's not just the brown cardigan. It's the total ignorance of social normality."

"Not now," said Friday, before going over to her father. "Dad, why were you looking for me? You never have before. Not even the time you left me at the mall, not realizing that I wasn't in the car."

"What?" said Dr. Barnes. "I don't recall the data to which you're referring."

Friday sighed. "Of course you don't. Just tell me, why are you here?"

"Oh," said Dr. Barnes. Suddenly his eyes welled with tears and his chin wobbled. "It's Dr. Barnes."

"Isn't that you?" asked Melanie.

"No, the other Dr. Barnes," said Dr. Barnes.

"Mom?" asked Friday.

"Yes, her," said Dr. Barnes.

"What's happened to Mom?" asked Friday.

"She's disappeared," said Dr. Barnes as he dissolved into sobs.

Friday took her father outside so he could compose himself. She sat him at a picnic table with a strategically placed box of tissues in front of him just in case he burst into tears again. Melanie and Ian stood by.

"What do you mean Mom's disappeared?" asked Friday. "She can't have stopped existing. She must be somewhere."

"All I know is that yesterday morning while I was eating breakfast I looked

$$+\Delta r\hat{T}_0 \frac{\hat{D}_2 \hat{T}_0}{2\hbar\alpha_r} \frac{1}{2}$$

$$\hat{D}^3 \frac{1}{2!} \frac{\hat{\Gamma}^3}{\hbar}$$

$$N$$

$$\Gamma^{(k+1)}_{n+1,j,l} \approx \exp$$

$$N^{(k)}_{n+1/2,j,l}$$

up and noticed she wasn't at the table!" said Dr. Barnes.

"That is a bad sign," Friday said, then turned to explain to her friends. "Mom never misses breakfast. She has an alarm set on her wristwatch to remind her when to eat."

"When I reflected on the available evidence, I realized I had no memory of her sitting at the table for dinner the night before," said Dr. Barnes. "So I investigated further and discovered she was nowhere in the house."

"Wow," said Friday, "and you noticed this in under twenty-four hours? I'm impressed."

"So I called her office at the university, and she wasn't there either," said Dr. Barnes. "I'm worried that she's been kidnapped!"

"Who would want to kidnap Mom?" asked Friday.

"Theoretical physics has all sorts of practical applications," said Dr. Barnes. "She might have been kidnapped by an arms manufacturer."

"Or aliens," said Melanie. "They like kidnapping people too."

"Have you called the police?" asked Ian.

"Why? Do you think they arrested her?" asked Dr. Barnes.

"No, to file a missing person report," said Friday.

"I hadn't thought of that," said Dr. Barnes. "Is that the type of thing police do? I'd hate to trouble them if it's not their field."

"Of course it's their field," said Friday.

"I think your father is even vaguer than I am," said Melanie.

"You should call the police right now," said Friday.

"All right," said Dr. Barnes. "Do you know their phone number?"

"Don't tell me you don't know the phone number for the emergency services," said Friday.

"Why?" asked Dr. Barnes. "Is it my birth date or something?"

"It's nine one one," said Friday.

"That's not my birthday," said Dr. Barnes.

"I'll call them," said Friday. "Then we can meet the police at your house. They'll want to search for evidence before the trail goes cold."

"I don't follow. The ambient temperature is pleasantly balmy," said Dr. Barnes. "I can't see why a trail would go cold."

"It's a figure of speech, Dad," said Friday. "I'm not literally talking about a low-temperature footpath."

"Really? Fascinating," said Dr. Barnes.

It was a two-hour drive to the Barneses' family home. Melanie went along with Friday, supposedly for emotional support, but really so she could get out of classes for the rest of the day. Friday tried questioning Dr. Barnes (her father) as he drove, but she had to give up because he was a terrible driver and it was distracting him too much. He nearly drove into an oncoming ice-cream truck while trying to remember what his wife had been wearing the last time he saw her. When they pulled up at the Barnes family's ordinary suburban home, the police were already there. They had marked off the whole front yard with crime scene tape.

"Oh my goodness!" exclaimed Dr. Barnes. "What's happened here?"

"Mother has gone missing," Friday reminded him. "We called the police about it two hours ago."

"And they've done all this already?" said Dr. Barnes. He was a university academic, so he was not used to anyone taking action with any degree of rapidity.

"Come on," said Friday. "Let's talk to the officer in charge."

They all got out of the car. Melanie and Dr. Barnes hung back while Friday ducked under the tape and started walking toward the front door.

"Stop right there!" snapped an angry-looking woman in a beige pantsuit. "If you take one more step, I'll arrest you."

Friday froze, one foot hovering midair.

"This is a crime scene," said the pantsuit woman. "With every step you take, you are contaminating the evidence."

"It may be a crime scene, but it's also my family home," said Friday, "and the missing person is my mother. If you allow me to put my foot down and continue walking into the building, I will probably be able to assist the officer in charge."

"*I* am the officer in charge," said the pantsuit woman. "My name is Detective Summers, and my experience with children is that they are anything but helpful."

"Well, you could have my father come in and have a look around to see what is missing or misplaced," said Friday. "But he is a theoretical physicist, with tenure, so he is about as aware of his physical surroundings as a dead geranium."

"That's ridiculous," said Detective Summers. "He's the victim's husband."

"Allow me to demonstrate," said Friday, turning to her father, who was still on the other side of the tape. "Dad, what day of the week is it?"

"What?" said Dr. Barnes.

"Do you know what day of the week it is?" repeated Friday.

"I suppose it's one of them," said Dr. Barnes. "I don't know . . . It will say on the calendar, I presume."

"Can you narrow it down?" asked Friday. "If you concentrate really hard, can you work out whether it is a weekday or a weekend?"

"How on earth could I be expected to know that?" asked Dr. Barnes.

"You just picked me up from school and classes were in session," said Friday. "So you should be able to deduce that it is a weekday."

"Oh yes, that line of reasoning does follow," agreed Dr. Barnes. "I hadn't really thought about it."

"What color are Mom's eyes?" continued Friday.

"Her eyes?" said Dr. Barnes. "Well, they're eye-colored, I suppose."

"Think hard, Dad," urged Friday. "You've been married for twenty-eight years. In all that time, have you ever looked at Mom and noticed what color her eyes were?"

"Blue . . . or maybe brown," said Dr. Barnes. "One of those two colors, I'd say."

"Behold my father's power of observation," said Friday.

"There must be an adult family member I can talk to," said Detective Summers.

"Yes, I do have four adult brothers and sisters," said Friday. "Quantum, Quasar, Halley, and Orion. They're all top physicists, too. You could get in touch with one of them."

"Oh no, you can't do that," said Dr. Barnes, shaking his head.

"Why not?" asked Friday.

"I tried already. I couldn't get hold of any of them this morning," said Dr. Barnes. "None of them answered the phone when I called. That's why I had to go and get Friday."

Friday was a little hurt. "I should have known I wouldn't be the first person you'd contact."

"So your four older children are missing as well?" asked Detective Summers. "And you didn't think to mention this before?"

"Could it be relevant?" asked Dr. Barnes.

Detective Summers looked like she wanted to slap Dr. Barnes. She took a deep breath, then turned to Friday. "Perhaps you had better be the one to come inside."

2

Inside the House

Friday wasn't allowed into the house until she was decked out in a full crime scene suit, which included white paper coveralls, white booties, a face mask, and a shower cap.

"You do realize that my fingerprints, hair, and skin cells will be all over the house already?" said Friday. "I did live here for eleven years."

"When it comes to evidence, you can never be too careful," said Detective Summers, leading Friday up the walkway. When she reached the front door she stopped and turned to Friday. For the first time Detective Summers had a look of compassion on her face. "Before we enter the house, I should warn you— what you see will be upsetting. Whoever took your mother made a real mess. The house has been completely turned upside down. They must have been searching for something. Your mother's research notes, perhaps. I know it can be distressing to see your family home violated."

A lump formed in Friday's throat. She nodded because she didn't think she could trust herself to speak. It wasn't until now that it occurred to her that the kidnapper might have handled her mother roughly.

Her mother might not have been the world's best mother. But she wasn't a bad person. Dr. Barnes lived in the theoretical world—she spent all her time inside her own mind, so to trick her into getting into a stranger's car would have been the easiest thing in the world. All you'd have to do was say, "Get in the car, Dr. Barnes, I'm here to take you to a conference," and she'd be halfway to Mauritius before it crossed her mind to wonder where she was going. Friday hoped the kidnappers hadn't hurt her mother.

Apart from being one of the world's leading scientists,

Dr. Barnes was Friday's mom. And she had only one mom. And she'd rather have a distracted, self-absorbed mother than no mother at all.

Detective Summers held open the front door and Friday stepped inside. She walked down the short corridor to the living room and then stopped. Three white-suited crime scene investigators were taking samples in the room, which was strange enough. It looked like aliens were paying an afternoon visit to her home. But as Friday looked around, she noticed the total dishevelment. There were papers and periodicals strewn everywhere. Cupboards hanging open, a broken mug on the kitchen floor, breakfast cereal trampled into the carpet, and a chair overturned. Friday took it all in.

"Are you all right?" asked Detective Summers.

"Of course I am," said Friday. "This is what the house always looks like."

"It is?!" asked Detective Summers.

"Well, not always," said Friday. "When I lived here, I used to tidy up after Mom and Dad as much as I could. But if I ever went away to camp or stayed with Uncle Bernie for a couple of days, the house would always look like this when I came back."

"But it looks like it's been ransacked," said Detective Summers.

"I know," agreed Friday. "Mom and Dad don't have very good life management skills. I really should have arranged some sort of caregiver to look after them when I moved out. What they really need is a nanny—someone to tell them when to eat, when to brush their teeth, and when to go to bed."

"Well, your mother's still missing," said Detective Summers.

"Plus your brothers and sisters. There must be something going on. If five of the nation's leading physicists have been kidnapped, that is going to be a huge deal."

"Are you sure she has been kidnapped?" asked Friday. "Perhaps there's another explanation."

"Yes, we're sure," said Detective Summers. "I didn't want to upset you or your father, but there was a note."

"From Mother?" asked Friday.

"Yes," said Detective Summers. "Whoever took her allowed her to leave a brief message."

"May I see it?" asked Friday.

Detective Summers looked doubtful. "You're a child. I don't want to do anything that might traumatize you. Police departments are forever getting sued for things like that."

"I won't sue," said Friday. "For starters, I'm not in touch enough with my emotions to be traumatized. The Barneses are big on suppressing all emotion. Just show me the note; I promise I'll be fine. At least for the foreseeable future. If I have any psychological repercussions, I'm sure they won't become apparent for years."

"All right," said Detective Summers, taking a plastic evidence bag out of her notebook. It looked like a sandwich bag, but it didn't contain a sandwich. It contained a crumpled handwritten note.

Friday took the bag carefully by the corner and inspected it closely.

"As you can see, the handwriting is barely legible," said Detective Summers. "She was clearly extremely distressed when she wrote it. Perhaps she had to do it in a hurry while her kidnappers weren't looking."

Friday peered closer. The letters barely looked like the standard Roman alphabet. It was as if they'd been furtively stabbed into the page, literally tearing up the paper fibers and blotting ink as she wrote.

"Can you make out what it says?" asked Detective Summers. "Our cryptographers have been working on it, but they haven't had much luck yet."

"Yes," said Friday. "It reads, *They are taking me away now. I tried to argue. They leave me no choice. I am being forced. Farewell.*"

"The poor woman," said Detective Summers.

"Hmm," said Friday. "May I have a look around to see if anything is missing?"

"Of course," said Detective Summers. She followed Friday into the bedroom. The bed was unmade. The drawers were hanging open and clothes were strewn about.

"You'll never be able to tell what's missing in all this mess," said Detective Summers.

Friday opened the wardrobe. There were very few clothes hanging inside. Just a couple of shirts. The wardrobe was mainly full of old scientific periodicals, which had been untidily stacked on the floor up to waist height.

"That's interesting," said Friday.

"What?" asked Detective Summers.

"Her dress is missing," said Friday.

"Which dress?" asked Detective Summers.

"Her *only* dress," said Friday. "Mother has no interest in clothes or fashion. She owns one navy-blue dress. For weddings, formal dinners, and things like that. And that one dress isn't here."

"What does that mean?" asked Detective Summers.

"I'm not sure," said Friday. "Let's take a look in the kitchen."

Friday led Detective Summers to the kitchen, where she opened a cupboard and took down a canister that said *Sugar* in blue print.

"What's sugar got to do with this?" asked Detective Summers.

"My mother doesn't believe in processed sugar," said Friday. "She never has it in the house." Friday opened the canister and looked inside. It was empty. "This is where she keeps her passport," said Friday.

"So the kidnapper took her passport?" said the detective. "This is serious. If she's been missing since yesterday, she could be anywhere in the world by now."

Friday stared into the canister. "I have a suspicion where my mother might be."

"Where?" asked Detective Summers.

"What's the date?" asked Friday.

"Sixteenth of October. Why?" asked Detective Summers.

Friday sighed. "Because the tenth of December is the anniversary of Alfred Nobel's death, and the traditional pre-ceremony lecture tour of Europe takes about seven weeks."

"What's that supposed to mean?" asked Detective Summers, looking baffled.

Friday strode across the front yard to confront her father. He was still waiting on the other side of the tape with Melanie.

"Dad, can you remember Mom mentioning something about her winning the Nobel Prize?" asked Friday.

"The Nobel Prize?" asked Dr. Barnes. "It doesn't ring a bell."

"She hasn't been planning a trip to Sweden, has she?" asked Friday.

"Sweden? Why would she go there?" asked Dr. Barnes.

"Because the Nobel Prizes are presented each year in Sweden on the tenth of December, the anniversary of Alfred Nobel's death," said Friday. "But the winners are announced much earlier, in October. Is there any chance Mom has not been kidnapped but has, in fact, simply flown to Europe for a lecture tour ahead of her acceptance of the Nobel Prize for Physics? And that Quantum, Quasar, Halley, and Orion have gone with her?"

"Now that you mention it," said Dr. Barnes, "your mother did say something about wanting me to go with her to some awards night. I must have missed the taxi when they all left."

"Was the taxi due to pick you up at seven forty-five last night?" asked Melanie.

"Yes!" said Dr. Barnes. "That's right, I remember now. How did you know?"

"Yes, how did you know?" asked Friday.

"It says seven forty-five on the back of Dr. Barnes's hand," said Melanie.

Dr. Barnes looked at his hand. "Oh yes! My secretary must have written it on there to help me to remember. She writes down all my important scheduling on my hand in permanent marker."

"But what about the note?" asked Detective Summers. "Your mother obviously wrote it in desperation. The handwriting alone showed that."

"No, actually that's Mom's regular handwriting," said Friday. "The clichés about mad scientists don't just come from nowhere. And you've got to realize that my mother is very clinical and ordered in the way she thinks and speaks. So her words—*They are taking me away now. I tried to argue. They leave me no choice. I am being forced. Farewell*—could simply mean the taxi is here, she had an argument with my brothers and sisters about sending the taxi away and waiting for Dad, she lost the argument, and they are setting out for the airport."

"I can't believe it," said Detective Summers. "All the time and resources wasted because some crazy academic is too vague to notice that his wife has gone to collect a Nobel Prize. This can't be happening to me. Are there hidden cameras somewhere? Is this a prank show?" Detective Summers looked around as if expecting a camera person to jump out of a bush.

"No, I'm afraid it's just regular day-to-day life in the Barnes household," said Friday.

"I ought to have you both arrested for wasting police time," said Detective Summers.

"Hey, I'm the one who figured it out for you," said Friday. "And shouldn't you be relieved that my mother hasn't been kidnapped?"

"I have real crimes I'm supposed to be investigating," said Detective Summers, "and I've just wasted four hours and goodness knows how much of our department's crime scene investigation budget on this."

"Those shower caps and paper booties are expensive, are they?" asked Melanie.

Detective Summers took out her phone and started dialing. "My boss is going to *looove* this," she muttered sarcastically as she walked away.

"I suppose we'd better get back to school," said Friday.

"But what about me?" asked Dr. Barnes.

"What do you mean, what about you?" said Friday. "We've established that Mother is all right. Quantum,

Quasar, Halley, and Orion will look after her. She's only going to be gone seven weeks."

"But who's going to look after me for seven weeks?" asked Dr. Barnes.

"What do you expect?" said Friday. "Do you want me to hire a babysitter to look after you?"

"Do you know anyone who would be interested?" asked Dr. Barnes optimistically.

"I was being sarcastic," said Friday. "You're a grown man. You should be able to look after yourself."

"But I never have before," said Dr. Barnes. "You can't expect me to take on a new role without a discussion, written instructions, and a training program." Dr. Barnes was starting to get very agitated. He looked like he might start crying.

"I think you might have to find a babysitter after all," said Melanie.

"This is ridiculous," said Friday. "I'm eleven years old. I can't be responsible for your well-being. I've got to get back to school."

"What about your uncle Bernie?" suggested Melanie.

"That buffoon!" exclaimed Dr. Barnes. "He's not staying here."

"They can't stand each other," explained Friday.

"But aren't they brothers?" asked Melanie.

"Exactly, that's why they can't stand each other," said Friday.

"We could take your dad with us," said Melanie. "If he was at Highcrest Academy, he'd get his meals and accommodation taken care of."

"I think Dad is a little bit too old to enroll as a student," said Friday.

"Of course," agreed Melanie. "But I'm sure the Headmaster would be happy to give Dr. Barnes a job. You know how much he hates the head of the science department. And it would really irritate Mr. Breznev if the Headmaster hired someone much more qualified to come and be a guest teacher."

"I guess that might work," conceded Friday. "But frankly, I'd rather not have my father hanging around at school."

"Why?" asked Melanie.

"Because, you know," said Friday awkwardly, "he'll cramp my style."

"Friday, I hate to break it to you," said Melanie, "but you have no style."

"True," conceded Friday.

"Besides," continued Melanie, "you've never been close with your parents. This could be an opportunity for you to get to know your father better."

"That's a nice thought," said Friday. "But I think I know him just well enough already."

"The only other alternative is that you take seven weeks off from school and come and live with him here," said Melanie.

Friday looked at her father. He was staring at his own shoes, no doubt lost in his own thoughts about physics.

"Me and Dad together in the house for seven weeks?!" Friday shuddered at the mental image this generated. "I'll call the Headmaster."

Half an hour later, Dr. Barnes was driving the two girls back to school. The Headmaster had been delighted to offer Dr. Barnes a short-term teaching position. The Parents Association would be impressed to have a man with two doctorates on staff, the teachers would be terrified that the new substitute teacher was wildly more qualified than any of them, and the students would be given an insight into just how much they didn't know about physics.

It was always good for teenagers to be reminded of the depths of their ignorance. The Highcrest Academy student body had, in the Headmaster's opinion, an unhealthily high level of self-esteem. Teenagers were meant to be awkward and self-conscious. It wasn't good for them to be allowed to think they knew everything. Convincing his students that they didn't know everything was usually an impossible task. You needed a jackhammer and wrecking bar to try to make the tiniest crack in their egos. The Headmaster hoped that Dr. Barnes would be that jackhammer.

"I've never been away from your mother for so long," worried Dr. Barnes.

"It's only seven weeks," said Friday.

"But what if she meets somebody?" asked Dr. Barnes.

"You're worried she'll fall in love with someone else?" asked Friday.

"Love?!" exclaimed Dr. Barnes. "Goodness, no. I hadn't thought of that. But I doubt she would. Doesn't sound like her."

"Then what are you worried about?" asked Melanie.

"What if she meets another physicist?" worried Dr. Barnes. "Someone with different insights, fresh theories. What if she starts collaborating on research papers with them, behind my back?"

"There are lots of fish in the sea," said Melanie. "Or,

in this case, physicists in the sea. You could collaborate with someone else, too."

Dr. Barnes shook his head. "I couldn't do it. There's only one scientist I want checking my algorithms—and that's Dr. Barnes."

Melanie looked to Friday. "Your father refers to his wife by her job title?"

"They think it's important to maintain formality," said Friday.

"I take everything back," said Melanie. "It's amazing you're as normal as you are."

"I know," agreed Friday. She patted her father on the hand. "Everything is going to be all right. You'll come and stay at the school for a few weeks while Mom finishes her lecture tour. The school will give you three square meals a day. It'll do you good." Friday turned to Melanie to explain. "Mom and Dad got scurvy last year from only eating instant noodles."

As they turned into the school's driveway Friday's heart warmed. It felt good to be coming home. Her actual childhood home, which they'd just come from, had always felt cold and empty to her. Here at Highcrest Academy she had a place, a function—plus she had access to hot meals. She felt safer just being inside the gates again.

"Why are there so many people standing on the front steps?" asked Melanie.

Friday's eyesight was not as good as Melanie's, but as they drew closer she could see that the entire student body was assembled on and around the front steps of the school.

"Could it be some sort of evacuation drill?" asked Friday.

"We had a real fire yesterday," Melanie reminded her, "so we won't be needing a fire drill again for ages."

"There's a sign hanging from the roof," said Friday. "Can you read it?"

"It says . . ." Melanie strained to see, the lettering getting larger as they grew nearer. "*Welcome.*"

"Do you think they've got the whole school out to welcome us back?" asked Friday. "We've only been gone for one afternoon."

"Also, we irritate people," added Melanie. "If they were going to put their feelings toward us on a banner, it would be more likely to read, *Oh, it's you.*"

"Wait, there's some smaller writing underneath," said Friday. "It says, *Welcome . . . Princess Ingrid.*"

Dr. Barnes pulled up in front of the main building. "Dad, you can't stop here," said Friday. "You need to park in the staff parking lot."

"I do?" said Dr. Barnes. "But there are so many people here. It would be rude not to say hello."

"Since when have you ever worried about being rude?" asked Friday.

There was a rap at the window. The Vice Principal was glaring in. "Kindly move your vehicle. We are waiting for a VIP!"

"A VIP?" asked Dr. Barnes. "Is that some sort of astronomical event, like an asteroid shower?"

"He means a very important person," explained Friday. "Come on, Dad, if you turn around the side of the building, the staff parking lot will be just ahead."

"Don't they have valet parking?" asked Dr. Barnes.

"Our school is fancy, but it's not that fancy," said Melanie.

"Oh, very well." Dr. Barnes stomped on the accelerator and turned the key, but nothing happened. He kept stomping on the accelerator. "It won't go!"

"That's because you've flooded the engine," said Friday. "Have you even had this car serviced since I left home?"

"You have to service a car?" asked Dr. Barnes.

"I'll take that as a *no*," said Friday. "Stop stomping on the accelerator. Give it a second and try again."

The Vice Principal was tapping on the window again. "You must move this car, now!" he ordered.

"We're trying," said Friday, "but the engine is flooded. If you want us to move, you'll have to push us."

Dr. Barnes was stomping on the accelerator again. "Dad, stop doing that, you're making it worse," said Friday.

In the distance they could hear police sirens. "They've called the police?" said Melanie. "The Vice Principal is getting very strict these days."

The car suddenly lunged forward. Friday looked around to see the entire football team pushing the car. Although they probably should have told Dr. Barnes what they were doing first because, being a deeply silly man, he panicked. He lifted his hands off the steering wheel and the car slowly veered in an arc, crashing into the marble statue of Socrates that stood alongside the driveway. The elderly car making contact with the hard marble made a loud *crunch*.

The police sirens were growing louder the whole time, which was a good thing because it drowned out the Vice Principal yelling at Dr. Barnes as they all got out of the wrecked car. Suddenly two police motorcycles swooped over the crest in the driveway and sped around the circular route to the front of the building. A long black limousine followed close behind.

The limousine parked right in front of the steps. The door opened and a large muscular man in a gray suit stepped out. He touched his ear as though listening on an earpiece and looked all around before stepping back to hold the rear door open.

For a moment nothing happened. Then a beautiful blond girl emerged from the car. She wore jeans, a short-sleeved blouse, a pink crystal

necklace, and pink sneakers—much the
same as any other student at the school
(except for Friday, who preferred ugly
brown cardigans). But even such ordinary clothes could not diminish the
fact that this girl was stunningly
gorgeous.

The Headmaster stepped forward
and bowed to the blond girl. Friday had never seen a grown
man who wasn't Japanese bow
before.

Socrates

"Welcome to Highcrest Academy, Your Highness," said the Headmaster.

"Your Highness?" Friday whispered to Melanie.

"She must be the princess," said Melanie.

"But this isn't a Disney movie," whispered Friday. "Princesses don't just pop up out of nowhere."

"No," agreed Melanie. "It would be alarming if they did."

Friday peered closer. "She must be . . . Princess Ingrid of Norway."

"What makes you say that?" asked Melanie.

"The necklace she's wearing. I've read that the Norwegian heir to the throne wears the Haakon Stone around their neck at all times," said Friday. "It's a tradition that dates back to the fourteenth century. The pink crystal would be a diamond."

"I didn't know diamonds were crystals," said Melanie.

"They're a type of crystal," said Friday. "Carbon so tightly compressed it forms a crystalline structure."

"On behalf of everyone here at Highcrest Academy, welcome to our school," the Headmaster formally announced.

The princess nodded her acknowledgment.

The Headmaster turned. "If you come with me, Your Highness, I will show you to your room."

The princess started to follow the Headmaster into the building. She ignored the three hundred students openly staring at her. But her eye caught the steaming car wreck pressed against the undamaged statue.

"What is this, I wonder?" asked the princess. She had a thick Norwegian accent. "Is it some sort of art-work? A public sculpture of found objects, perhaps?"

The Headmaster looked at the car wreck. "Yes, it is a metaphor for how I feel at the end of a long term."

Suddenly there was a loud *bang* from the engine. The hood buckled up and smoke began to pour out from the sides. There was a flash of movement as the body-guard rushed across the driveway and slammed into Ian, knocking over a dowdy girl behind him.

"Hey, I didn't do anything!" protested Ian.

"It's all right," called Friday, stepping forward to in-tervene. "It's just a poorly maintained car with leaking flammable fluids. Nothing sinister."

"Sorry, my mistake," said the bodyguard, straight-ening himself up. "I thought I saw the boy acting sus-piciously."

"It wouldn't be the first time," said Melanie.

"I was just standing here," argued Ian. "She's the one who brought the dangerous automobile with the lunatic driver." He pointed at Friday.

The Headmaster glared at her. "Barnes, Pelly, wait for me outside my office."

"We didn't do anything," protested Friday.

But the Headmaster had already turned and was leading Princess Ingrid into the main building. As soon as they disappeared inside, the assembled students started chattering excitedly among themselves.

"Right, all of you," yelled the Vice Principal, "get back to class!"

The student body started to disperse, except for Ian, who sidled over to Friday.

"Quite an entrance," he said.

"I wasn't the one driving," said Friday.

"No, but the apple doesn't fall far from the tree, does it?" said Ian.

Dr. Barnes was staring at the caved-in front of his car, as if he couldn't work out how it had happened. Friday noticed he was wearing a brown cardigan that was almost identical to her own. She sighed. "I don't think Dad is used to seeing the practical application of physics at such close hand." She raised her voice to call out to him, "Force equals mass times acceleration, hey, Dad?"

"What?" said Dr. Barnes looking up. "Yes, I suppose so, but I don't understand why anyone would put a statue right here."

"I think they expect you to drive around it, sir," said Ian. "By staying on the driveway."

Dr. Barnes looked down at his feet. The tires of his car had cut big gashes into the lawn. "Yes, my car breached protocol." He nodded as if that explained it. "I suppose I'd better find my quarters." Dr. Barnes wandered off. Having come to terms with how the accident had occurred, it did not cross his mind that he should take responsibility for the removal of the car.

"I can see why you wanted to come to boarding school," Melanie said to Friday sympathetically. "Looking after your father is like looking after a pet. Except you can't lock him in the backyard."

5

The Headmaster's Troubles

Friday and Melanie sat outside the Headmaster's office for a long time. Melanie used the opportunity to catch up on sleep. She'd already had a ninety-minute nap during the car ride, but Melanie never let a little thing like being well rested stop her from slipping off to sleep again. Friday privately suspected that her roommate had not entirely recovered from being bitten by a tsetse fly the previous summer.

Friday used the opportunity to reflect on her busy morning. It wasn't every day that her mother became a Nobel laureate, a princess enrolled in her school, and she was involved in a car accident. She noted that she was starting to feel one of the classic symptoms that followed any adrenaline rush—sleepiness. But unlike Melanie, Friday was unable to get comfortable on the bench. She was just considering lying down on the floor when the Headmaster bustled into view at the end of the corridor. Friday elbowed Melanie in the ribs.

"What?" asked Melanie drowsily.

"The Headmaster's here," said Friday.

"He'll be more interested in talking to you," said Melanie. "Wake me if he wants me." She closed her eyes and fell into a deep sleep again.

Friday stood to meet the Headmaster.

"Inside," he snapped.

Friday followed him into his office, shutting the door behind her.

"You had to mess everything up, didn't you?" said the Headmaster.

"What?" asked Friday.

"The princess's bodyguard is all worked up," said

the Headmaster. "He thinks your father's crashing into the statue was a terrorist attack."

"He's just a bad driver," said Friday.

"Yes, I finally convinced Mr. Rasmus of that," said the Headmaster. "I introduced him to your father, and it was immediately self-evident that he wasn't capable or coherent enough to have a political ideology. But still, couldn't you have let me have one quiet afternoon? I get a princess from the Norwegian royal family to enroll here for six weeks, which is a huge coup for the school. It's the best publicity we've ever had. And the first day is blighted by a traffic accident."

"No one will know," said Friday. "There wasn't any press around."

"Word will get out," said the Headmaster. "I might have banned all electronic devices from the school, but I can't stop students from writing letters. This isn't a prisoner-of-war camp."

"I think some of the parents would be happier if it were," said Friday. "Why did a Norwegian princess want to come to our school anyway? Has she done something wrong in her homeland? Has she been banished?"

"Banished?!" exclaimed the Headmaster. "I forbid

you to start that rumor. No, she *wanted* to come here. Our school's polo program is the second best in the world."

"Why didn't she want to go to the school with the best polo program?" asked Friday.

"It's in Argentina," explained the Headmaster. "The king wouldn't have allowed that. You've seen how pretty the princess is. If she was surrounded by Argentinean polo players, she'd soon run off with one of them. It's what princesses always do in romance novels."

"I'll have to take your word for it," said Friday.

"She's here to compete in the Trumpley Cup, our annual match against Pontworth Manor Preparatory School," said the Headmaster. "It's the highest level of high school polo played in the country."

"I wouldn't have thought there was much high school polo played in the country," said Friday. "It must be right up there with competitive . . . flushing enormous amounts of money down the toilet."

"Look, I'm very pleased to have your father here," said the Headmaster. "Having a scientist of his caliber on the staff will look very good in the prospectus, but I expect you to keep an eye on him and keep him out of trouble. It's probably a good thing he has smashed his car. He won't be able to accidentally run over any students now."

"But he's my father," said Friday. "He's not my responsibility. I'm supposed to be *his* responsibility."

"Do you really wish your roles were reversed?" asked the Headmaster.

"No, I suppose not," said Friday. "All right, I'll keep an eye on him."

"Good," said the Headmaster, standing up. "I've got a meeting. There's another girl starting today. Poor thing, no one is going to notice she's arrived. She just got knocked over by Mr. Rasmus when he was crash-tackling Ian. Still, I have to give her the standard welcome talk." The Headmaster glanced at his watch, or, rather, he glanced at his wrist because his watch wasn't there.

"Where's my watch?" asked the Headmaster.

"Did you put it on this morning?" asked Friday.

"Of course," said the Headmaster. "I always wear a watch. You know how much I enjoy chiding people for being tardy."

"Was the strap old?" asked Friday. "Could it have fallen off?"

"No, it was a new strap and a new watch," said the Headmaster. "It can't have broken. It's one of those fancy new computer watches that can take photos and record conversations."

"Then there's only one alternative," said Friday.

"What?" asked the Headmaster.

"Someone stole it," said Friday.

"That's just what I need!" said the Headmaster.

"On the same day that a royal princess arrives, one of the students decides to become a thief."

"Or one of the teachers," said Friday.

"And the princess is wearing the Haakon Stone," said the Headmaster. "It's almost more valuable than she is. I wish I could just put her and her necklace in a vault so I'd know they were safe."

"Perhaps your watch was stolen because of something you recorded on it," said Friday. "An incriminating photograph or conversation."

"Well, I know I had it on when I was waiting for the princess to arrive, because I kept checking it," said the Headmaster.

"It isn't easy to steal a watch right off someone's wrist," said Friday. "You need to get very close, and you need to distract your target."

"But I would have noticed," said the Headmaster.

"Who have you shaken hands with?" asked Friday.

"Um . . ." said the Headmaster, "the princess . . . her bodyguard . . . the other new girl . . . your father . . ."

"Well, my father wouldn't have done it," said Friday.

"I don't see how he is a less likely suspect than a royal princess," said the Headmaster.

"What about Ian Wainscott?" asked Friday.

"Your boyfriend?" asked the Headmaster.

"He's not my boyfriend," protested Friday.

"It's all right," said the Headmaster. "It's not against school rules. You're allowed to have a boyfriend."

"But I don't," said Friday.

"Well, you're always together," said the Headmaster. "If it looks like a duck and it quacks like a duck—"

"It's a duck, not a boyfriend," interrupted Friday.

"All right, all right," said the Headmaster. "No need to get snappy with me."

"Sorry," said Friday. "I just mentioned Ian because he can do sleight-of-hand magic. He knows how to lead the eye."

"Well, I didn't shake hands with him," said the Headmaster. "Although, now that you mention it, he did grab my sleeve to catch my attention when he spotted you coming up the driveway."

"Typical," said Friday.

"But a lot of students were standing close by," said the Headmaster. "I was distracted. Any one of them might have taken it."

"Let me see your wrist," said Friday.

"Why?" asked the Headmaster.

"Because it's the scene of the crime," said Friday, taking her magnifying glass out of her pocket.

The Headmaster felt uncomfortable having a student take him by the hand and inspect him so closely.

"Tsk, tsk, tsk," said Friday.

"What?" asked the Headmaster.

"According to this school's anaphylaxis policy, no one is meant to have nut products on school grounds," said Friday. "But from the brown stain on your cuff, I can see you ate peanut butter for breakfast." She sniffed his cuff. "Yes, definitely peanut butter."

The Headmaster snatched his hand away. "Must you sniff everything?"

"Let me have another look," said Friday. "Come on, you know it's in your best interest if I find any clues."

The Headmaster reluctantly held out his hand, again.

Friday looked at the back of his wrist, then turned it over and looked at the inside. She carefully inspected every centimeter. The red compression marks where the band had been were still clearly visible, so the watch had not been gone for long. "You're very lucky, Head-master," said Friday.

"Why?" said the Headmaster. "How can I be lucky when I've just lost an expensive watch?"

"Because you could have easily had a very nasty accident," said Friday. "Whoever stole your watch was able to do it so swiftly and unnoticed because they cut it off with something extremely sharp."

"How do you know that?" asked the Headmaster.

"Look," said Friday, handing her magnifying glass to him. "The hair on one side of your wrist has been shaved off right here." She pointed to a small, smooth spot on the side of the Headmaster's wrist.

"What?" said the Headmaster.

"Your watch was cut off with a razor-sharp blade," said Friday. "If the thief had misjudged even slightly, he or she might have severed your artery, causing you to rapidly lose a massive amount of blood."

The Headmaster turned pale. "Who would do such a thing?"

"Someone careless, carefree, or desperate," said Friday. "Would you like me to get to the bottom of it?"

"I'd like my watch back," said the Headmaster.

"I'll investigate," said Friday.

"Before you go, Barnes," said the Headmaster, "there's something you should know."

"That sounds ominous," said Friday.

"You've got a new next-door neighbor," said the Headmaster.

Chapter

6

The Next-Door Neighbor

"The Royal Princess of Norway is next door?" whispered Melanie. She and Friday were standing in their own dorm room.

"That's right," whispered Friday.

"But I just bumped into another girl coming out of that room," said Melanie. "A short, dowdy girl with dark brown hair, wearing a misshapen blue cardigan."

"No, that's the other new girl. They're roommates," said Friday.

"Well, I like the dowdy girl in the blue cardigan," said Melanie. "She

reminded me of you, although her cardigan wasn't quite as ugly as yours. It's a nicer color, for starters."

"The Headmaster put the princess in the room next door to ours so I can keep an eye on her," said Friday.

"Hasn't she got a bodyguard who can do that?" asked Melanie.

"Yes, but his room is on the boys' floor," said Friday. "It wouldn't be appropriate to have a great big man living in a dormitory full of girls."

"I can only imagine the giggling it would cause," agreed Melanie.

"Do you think I would be invading her privacy if I pressed my ear to the wall and tried to hear what she's doing in there?" asked Friday.

"Oh yes, definitely," said Melanie. "But we're pre-teen girls. We're supposed to have a cavalier disregard for the sensitivities of our peers."

They both pressed their ears against the wall. "Can you hear anything?" asked Friday.

"No, the wall is not very forthcoming," said Melanie.

"That's the problem with attending an elite preparatory academy," said Friday. "The buildings are so well built, the walls are solid brick and plaster. If this were a state school with drywall, we'd be able to hear her breathing."

"If this were a state school," said Melanie, "the heir to the throne of Norway would not be living in the room next to us."

There was a knock at the door.

"That might be the princess," said Melanie. "Perhaps that's why we can't hear her through the wall—because she's outside the door."

Friday opened the door and immediately guessed that this was the other new girl standing before her. She was wearing an eye-catchingly drab blue cardigan.

"Hello," said the new girl as she nervously shifted her glasses higher up her nose. "I'm, um . . ."

"The new girl?" asked Friday.

"Gosh, yes," said the new girl. "I heard you were good at deducing things. I didn't realize you'd start doing it right away."

"This is Debbie," said Melanie. "Debbie, meet Friday."

"I've never met anybody named after a day of the week before," confessed Debbie.

"That's because most parents are a great deal more sensible than mine," said Friday.

"Would you like to come in and listen to the wall?" asked Melanie.

"All right," said Debbie.

The three girls pressed their ears against the wall.

"What are we listening for?" asked Debbie.

"Your new roommate, the princess," said Melanie.

"Oh," said Debbie.

"But she's disappointingly quiet," said Friday, stepping away.

"I actually came over because I thought you might

be able to help me with something, if it's not too much trouble. I don't want to bother you if you're busy," said Debbie.

"We're listening to a wall," said Friday. "You can't get any less busy than that."

"Unless you take a nap," added Melanie.

"So what's the problem?" said Friday. "Lost property? Missing homework? Or has someone falsely accused you of a crime?"

"Nothing that exciting, I'm afraid," admitted Debbie. "I've just locked myself out of my room. I'm not used to having a key to keep track of, you see."

"That's easily fixed," said Friday, going to her desk and taking out her lock-picking kit. "Fortunately the school has cheap, substandard locks on all the dormitory doors. It will only take me a few minutes to pick it for you."

"And I'll lend you a shoelace," said Melanie.

"A shoelace?" asked Debbie.

"So when you find your key you can tie it around your neck." Melanie pulled a shoelace with a key on it out from under her sweater. "I have a problem with that sort of thing, too. Before Friday became my roommate I once slept in the hallway for three nights because I lost my key and didn't want to bother anyone about it."

"I've already got one," said Debbie, taking a length of leather string out from under her shirt. It had a pebble with a hole in the middle strung on it. "Technically, it's not a shoelace but a leather necklace. Same idea, though."

"What type of stone is that?" asked Melanie.

"It's just a pebble," said Debbie. "My family's not big on fancy jewelry."

By the time Melanie and Debbie wandered out into the hallway, Friday had the tension wrench inserted in the lock and was working on the first tumbler.

"Where did you learn how to do that?" asked Debbie.

"At home," said Friday. "I came home from school one day and found the house locked up. My parents had gone to a conference in Kuala Lumpur and had forgotten to tell me. But I was able to fashion a tension wrench out of a screwdriver and a pick out of a hairpin, and in just two short hours I taught myself how to pick a lock."

"Excuse me," said a heavily accented voice.

Friday looked up to see Princess Ingrid glaring down her nose at her. She was even more beautiful close up, even from that angle. Most people don't look their best when you're staring up their nose. But this princess looked stunning. She also looked deeply un-impressed.

"Yes?" said Friday.

"You are in the way of my access," said the princess.

"Sorry," said Friday.

"I am guiding the entrance of my possessions," said the princess.

Friday looked around the princess and saw another gorgeous blond-haired person behind her. Ian Wainscott was holding one end of her massive traveling trunk.

"Hello, Friday," said Ian. "Fancy meeting you here, on your hands and knees, trying to break in. What a surprise."

"Is this some miscreant?" the princess asked Ian. "Should we inform the police officers?"

"The police are already aware of her movements," said Ian, shaking his head sadly. "Hers is more of a mental health issue than an actual crime."

"Ah," said the princess, "I understand. She is, how you say . . . bonkers?"

"Quite right," agreed Ian.

"Hello there, Mel," said a voice.

"Binky, is that you?" asked Melanie.

Binky Pelly bent sideways so they could see his head around the side of the trunk. He was holding the other end. "Yes, it's me. Wainscott needed something carried. And when you need something heavy lugged, I'm your man."

Binky was Melanie's older brother. He was an affable if dim-witted boy. He was also very large and muscular.

"You will move now so that my trunk, she will be installed," the princess said to Friday.

"As it is your first day and English is your second language, I shall overlook your pronoun misuse and do as you ask," said Friday, getting up and standing back.

The princess unlocked the door with her key, and the boys moved forward with the trunk. The princess stopped them at the doorway. "You may go now," she announced, before grabbing the handle of the trunk herself, rolling it into the room, and slamming the door.

"Nice girl," said Binky happily.

"Do you think so?" asked Ian.

"Well, obviously not in manners, or the way she talks or treats people," said Binky. "But very nice to look at."

"One out of four isn't too bad," said Friday.

"Exactly," said Binky. "Much better than none out of four."

Debbie tried the door handle. "It's unlocked. I can get in."

Then, in a very odd move, Debbie slid into the room she shared with the princess, keeping the door as closed as absolutely possible so that the others only got the smallest glimpse of the room behind her.

"Thanks for your help," said Debbie, her lips only just visible through an inch-wide crack in the door. "I'd invite you in, but there's a lot of dirty underwear lying around." She shut the door firmly.

"That was odd, wasn't it?" said Friday, turning to Melanie. "How can there be dirty underwear lying around? She only just got here."

"Maybe she brought some from home," said Ian.

"It certainly seemed odd to me," agreed Melanie. "And I've got a high benchmark of oddness to compare it to."

Chapter 7
A Dangerous Letter

Several days later Friday was sitting in geography class, totally ignoring the lesson. She already knew as much as she wanted to know about the imports and exports of Borneo. So Friday sat in the back row reading a Dorothy L. Sayers murder mystery in which the victim had died from being forced to listen to loud bell-ringing. Friday found this highly improbable. If loud, unpleasant noises could kill a person, people would be dropping dead from proximity to leaf blowers all the time.

"BARNES!"

Friday's head snapped up. Mr. Maclean was glaring at her. Everyone in the room had turned around to stare at her. Mr. Maclean had evidently been calling her name for some time.

"Timber and palm oil," said Friday.

"What?" asked Mr. Maclean.

"The chief exports of Borneo," said Friday. "Isn't that what we're discussing?"

"No," said Mr. Maclean. "I have a note here saying that you are required immediately in the library."

"What have I done now?" asked Friday.

"I don't know," said Mr. Maclean. "Maybe you've irritated the librarian as much as you've irritated me."

"I doubt it," said Friday. "I'm banned from entering the library, so she doesn't get to spend as much time with me as you do."

"Lucky her," said Mr. Maclean.

Friday got up and started packing her things into her bag. Melanie did the same.

"Where do you think you're going, Pelly?" asked Mr. Maclean.

"With Friday," said Melanie. "I didn't think you'd

miss me. I wasn't paying attention to what you were saying anyway."

Mr. Maclean rolled his eyes. "Don't any of you have any appreciation for the subject of geography?"

"Of course we do," said Melanie kindly. "We appreciate that it is nowhere near as unpleasant as math."

Friday and Melanie were soon hurrying across the quadrangle. The truth was, Mr. Maclean was almost as apathetic as Melanie, so he was quite glad to have two fewer students to teach for the remainder of the lesson. As they came to the turn in the landing, Friday looked up to see the librarian standing outside the door waiting for them. The librarian had taken an intense dislike to Friday from the moment she had met her. Over the months, getting to know Friday's personality had only made matters worse. Friday assumed she would be yelled at for some misdemeanor, and that the librarian was waiting outside so that Friday would not be allowed to sully the interior of the library with her presence. What the librarian actually said came as a complete shock.

"At last. You're here."

"You're happy to see me?" asked Friday.

"Obviously not," said the librarian. "You're still the most obnoxious child in the school. But I need your help."

"You've got a funny way of asking for it," said Melanie. "Usually when people want something, they are nice about it."

"It's all right, Melanie," said Friday. "It's a long way to ratchet your emotions down from intense hatred all the way to nice. If I'm not mistaken, the librarian has, with some struggle, managed to subdue her feelings from hatred down to loathing. I'm prepared to give her credit for her effort."

"You don't make it easy," said the librarian, rubbing her forehead. "Just hearing your voice makes my chest spasm with rage."

"Why don't we focus on the problem, then?" said Friday. "How can I help you?"

"Mr. Henderson had his eleventh-grade aerodynamics class in here," said the librarian. "And when they left, a letter had gone missing. I need you to find that letter."

"A letter?" said Melanie. "You mean written on paper? I didn't know people still did that."

"It's an old letter," said the librarian. "A valuable

collector's item. It was a letter written by Marie Curie."

Friday gasped. "I love Marie Curie!"

"Really?" said Melanie. "But I thought you loved Ian Wainscott?"

"No, Marie Curie was an early-twentieth-century scientist," said Friday. "She's my role model. She won two Nobel Prizes. One for physics and one for chemistry. She also drove a van around the front lines in World War I, giving injured soldiers X-rays—a technology only possible thanks to her breakthrough in isolating radium and polonium. And in perhaps her greatest breakthrough for women's rights, she arranged free child care for herself—by getting her father-in-law to look after her children."

"Oh, that Marie Curie," said Melanie, nodding. "I've seen pictures of her. She's the one whose hair looked like a bird's nest made by a very angry bird."

"Yes, that's her," agreed Friday.

"Well, the school had a letter handwritten by her," said the librarian. "And it's gone."

"What was the letter about?" asked Friday.

"It was a letter to the Nobel Prize Committee," said the librarian. "They'd asked her not to attend the awards ceremony in person because they thought the way she was conducting her personal life was scandalous. So she wrote them a very rude letter back."

"Were there swear words?" asked Melanie.

"I don't know," said the librarian. "I don't speak French. But there was a graphic description of where they could put their Nobel Prize—which demonstrated that Marie Curie had an impressive knowledge of anatomy as well as physics and chemistry."

"It sounds like a really good letter," said Friday. "Of course I'll help you find it. Could you explain how it came to be missing?"

"Usually it's kept locked in the archives," said the librarian. "We wouldn't want students to get anywhere near it."

"Heaven forbid they might learn something," said Friday.

"But the head of science asked me to get it out so he could show it to your father," said the librarian. "He thought Dr. Barnes would be interested."

"Poor naïve Mr. Breznev," said Friday, shaking her head. "Little does he realize that my father is such a snob when it comes to physics that he considers Marie Curie to be a chemist and therefore a second-rate hack."

"Anyway," continued the librarian, "I got the letter out and put it on the circulation desk, ready for Mr. Breznev to collect it. Then I continued about my duties. Five minutes later, when Mr. Breznev came to pick it up, the letter was gone."

"Could it have blown away?" asked Friday. "In a gust from the door?"

"No," said the librarian. "I set a stapler on top of the letter so it couldn't blow away. Someone must have moved the stapler intentionally and picked the letter up."

"But who would want to steal a letter by Marie Curie?" asked Melanie.

"I would," said Friday.

The librarian and Melanie looked at her.

"But of course I didn't," said Friday. "I didn't even know the school had one."

"So it must be some other obsessive science nerd," said Melanie.

"Your father," said the librarian.

"Dad wouldn't steal," said Friday.

"Are you sure about that?" asked the librarian.

When Friday thought about it, she realized she wasn't really sure. She spent so little time with her father she didn't really have any insight into what motivated him.

"He's certainly obsessive about science," said Friday. "But I don't know that he is materialistic enough to want to own a specific artifact."

"Didn't you say he bought Einstein's toothbrush in an online auction?" asked Melanie.

"Yes," conceded Friday, "but that was only because his own toothbrush had worn out and he needed a new one. It didn't occur to him that a toothbrush from the supermarket might be cheaper."

"Maybe someone stole the letter because they wanted to sell it for the money," suggested Melanie.

"But so few students here need money," said Friday.

"Except Ian," said Melanie. "With his father in jail and his assets frozen, Ian could use the cash."

"Yes," said Friday, "an obviously valuable letter just sitting in the open would be quite a temptation. But I don't think he would."

"Because you love him even more than you love Marie Curie?" said Melanie.

"No, because students don't have Internet access," said Friday. "He'd have no way to sell it."

"Well, it's gone and someone took it," said the librarian.

"Maybe it was the Pimpernel," said Melanie.

"Who?" asked Friday.

"The Pimpernel," said Melanie. "That's what everyone is calling the thief who's been stealing everything, because they're so elusive. No one has seen them and no one knows their identity."

"That's an unexpectedly literate reference for the students here," said Friday. "I wouldn't have thought anyone had read *The Scarlet Pimpernel*."

"Of course not," said Melanie. "But last year, before you came to Highcrest, the Headmaster showed the film version in the dining hall as an end-of-semester treat."

"But the Scarlet Pimpernel left a calling card," said Friday. "This thief hasn't been leaving calling cards."

"Perhaps our Pimpernel fell asleep before they got to that bit in the movie," said Melanie.

"Not everyone naps as much as you," said Friday.

"I know," said Melanie. "But they should try it. It's very nice."

"While it gratifies me that you're having a literary discussion," said the librarian, "can you please get on with the investigation?"

"Of course. We'd better inspect the scene of the crime," said Friday.

They all stepped into the library. Friday could immediately see the pink-and-black stapler sitting on the circulation desk.

"The letter was right there," said the librarian.

"Who was in the library at the time?" asked Friday.

"Just Mr. Henderson and his eleventh-grade aerodynamics class," said the librarian. "The students were taking a test. Mr. Henderson couldn't use his own classroom because he had dropped a thermometer in there and a hazmat team was called in to remove the mercury."

"Mr. Henderson is very passionate about science," said Friday. "He must have been your first suspect."

"He was," agreed the librarian. "But I noticed the letter was missing before he left, and I searched him thoroughly before I let him go."

"How thoroughly?" asked Friday.

"Very, very," said the librarian.

"Are you allowed to do that?" asked Melanie.

"It's my library," said the librarian. "I make the rules."

"But surely you're still subject to normal laws of human rights," said Melanie.

"Humans can forfeit their rights in my library," said the librarian. "They do so all the time."

Friday made a mental note that the librarian was clearly more insane than she had previously realized.

"May I see your wastebasket?" asked Friday.

"What for?" asked the librarian.

"I'm looking for evidence," said Friday.

The librarian showed Friday the wastebasket at the end of the circulation desk. It was a large round bin full of crumpled paper. Friday peered inside, then picked up the whole bin and tipped the contents all over the desk.

"What are you doing?" demanded the librarian. "Look at the mess you've made!"

"You want me to find the letter, don't you?" said Friday.

"But it won't be in there!" said the librarian. "Nobody would steal it and then throw it away."

"No," agreed Friday, "but that's not what I'm looking for. Aha! Here we go . . ." Friday picked up a scrunched-up ball of paper and started flattening it out.

"What is it?" asked Melanie.

"The aerodynamics test," said Friday. She glanced through the questions.

"What are you looking for?" asked the librarian.

"A motive," said Friday. She turned the page over to read the last question. "Oh no. This isn't good."

"What is it?" asked the librarian.

"The last question," said Friday, turning the paper around so that the librarian could read it. "It asks the student to design a paper airplane."

"I don't see the significance—" The librarian broke off when she did see the significance. "But they wouldn't, surely . . . ?"

"The letter was lying there on the desk," said Friday. "It was in French. Most students don't read French. They barely read English. Teenagers are thoughtless. They would have been talking among themselves about the exam, discussing the last question. One of them spots the piece of paper on the desk and, without a second thought, picks it up to test their design."

The librarian clasped her hand to her mouth. "That's horrifying. But if a student folded it and made it into a paper airplane, then they would have . . ." She swallowed, struggling to say the words. "Thrown it."

"Launched it, yes," agreed Friday.

"It could be anywhere by now," said the librarian.

"Yes," said Friday. "But it will be easy to find."

"It will?" asked Melanie. "One piece of paper in the entire school grounds?"

"Yes," said Friday, "because it wasn't an ordinary

piece of paper. It was a letter by Marie Curie. The first person to isolate radium. Her daily work constantly exposed her to radiation. She didn't realize the danger. It killed her in the end. And her papers—everything she wrote in her laboratory—are, to this very day, still radioactive. In France, her notebooks are kept in a lead-lined box."

"But I picked it up!" exclaimed the librarian.

"Yes, you did," said Friday. "You should probably wash your hands."

The librarian ran for the bathroom.

"So how are we going to find it?" asked Melanie.

"The way you can find anything radioactive," said Friday. "With a Geiger counter."

"Let me guess," said Melanie. "You've got one in your backpack?"

"As it happens, I do," said Friday.

Letter Tracking

The girls were soon tracking the radiation signature across the school. Friday was concentrating hard on the Geiger counter's dial as the needle flickered back and forth. When she got to the center of the quad she froze, turning first one way then another.

"What's the problem?" asked Melanie.

"There appear to be two radiation readings," said Friday.

BEE BEEP
BEE BEEP

"Do you think the school could own two letters by Marie Curie?" asked Melanie.

"I doubt it," said Friday. "But there's no way of telling which reading is coming from the letter."

"Sure there is," said Melanie. "We'll just have to do eenie, meenie, miney, mo."

"I've studied postgraduate-level probability," said Friday. "I'm not using eenie, meenie, miney, mo to make decisions."

"Why?" asked Melanie. "Are you worried it will make better life decisions than you? I bet eenie, meenie, miney, mo wouldn't have let you choose that cardigan for a start."

"Let's go this way," said Friday, following the radiation reading that led toward the social science building.

"You did eenie, meenie, miney, mo silently in your head, didn't you?" said Melanie.

"I did not," said Friday, blushing.

"I can tell when you're lying," said Melanie as she followed her.

The reading led them right up to the door of a storage room.

"Well, there's definitely something radioactive in there," said Friday.

"Should we get a hazmat team?" asked Melanie.

"It's not that radioactive," said Friday. "There's radio-active material in smoke detectors, and people don't avoid those."

"I do," said Melanie. "Horrible, noisy things. I'd rather be in a fire."

"I'm going to kick the door down," said Friday.

"Why don't you pick the lock?" asked Melanie.

"There's no time for that," said Friday. "Who knows what damage they could be doing to the letter as we speak? They could be folding extra air-foils and tearing bits off to alter the weight bal-ance."

"Do you even know how to kick down a door?" asked Melanie as Friday took a few steps back.

"Of course I do," said Friday. "I read all about it online. It's just a matter of simple physics. Mass times acceleration plus the force of momentum meeting a stationary object. Oh, and you have to yell really loudly to focus your chi."

"Isn't that a type of tea?" said Melanie.

"No, you're thinking of chai," said Friday. "Your chi is your energy."

"Okay," said Melanie, "I'll put my fingers in my ears and you can yell as loud as you want."

"Hiiyaaaaahhhh!" screamed Friday as she launched herself forward and slammed the ball of her foot into the door just below the lock. The lock smashed out through the frame, splintering the wood. The door flung open, and Friday, overbalanced, landed flat on her face. The door hit the wall hard and bounced back, whacking Friday on the side of her head.

"Ow," said Friday.

"Hello, Mr. Maclean," said Melanie.

"What on earth are you doing here?" demanded Mr. Maclean.

Friday looked up to see Mr. Maclean wearing nothing but a swimsuit and sun goggles as he struggled to sit up on a tanning bed. Ultraviolet light from the tanning bed bathed the room.

"I think we've found our radiation source," said Friday.

"Why? Do you think Mr. Maclean was reading Marie Curie's letter as he lay on the tanning bed?" asked Melanie.

"Excuse me," said Mr. Maclean, clutching a towel to his beige-colored chest. "A man has a right to a suntan, doesn't he?"

"I don't think that's one of the legal rights listed in the Constitution," said Friday. "But I certainly don't think it is illegal, either. Just strange and extremely vain to be secretly acquiring one in a closet."

"Well, I have to unwind somehow after an hour of seventh-grade geography," said Mr. Maclean.

"Oh, is geography over?" asked Melanie. "That's a shame. That means we're missing music now. I have some of my best naps in music."

"We've got to find that letter," said Friday. "We'll have to double back and trace the other reading."

Soon Friday and Melanie were using the Geiger counter again to follow the radiation reading across the school.

"It seems to be leading toward the administration building," said Melanie.

"Of course!" said Friday. "The clock tower."

They both looked up to see the tallest structure in the school: the clock tower. It was the architectural centerpiece of the administration building.

"It would be the perfect place to launch a paper airplane," said Friday.

"Oh dear," said Melanie. "It's a windy day. That letter could end up anywhere."

"We've got to get up there!" said Friday.

Unfortunately Friday and Melanie were even worse at running up a spiral staircase than they were at running in a straight line. It took some time, and a lot of gasping for breath, before they arrived at the top. Friday flung open the door only to have it thrown back at her by the force of the wind, the door hitting her in the forehead.

"Ow!" said Friday.

"At least it was a different part of your head this time," said Melanie. "Better to have two small lumps than one big one."

"Tell that to my cerebellum," said Friday. She clambered to her feet and looked out over the railing. Three boys were sitting on the far end of the top of the roof. They each had a paper airplane in their hand. One of the airplanes was the distinctive pale blue of early-twentieth-century French stationery.

"One . . . two . . ." began the boys.

"Nooooo!" cried Friday.

"Three!"

The boys launched their paper airplanes. One spun in a loop-de-loop, and a gust of wind pushed it back so that it hit its owner in the eye. Another airplane flew out a few feet; then the weight of the nose tipped it over, and it spiraled straight down to the ground.

But the fine quality of French paper meant that Marie Curie's letter fared much better in aeronautical form. The crisp folds and firm weight of the stationery helped the paper airplane pierce the air and be carried by a powerful gust out over the school.

"What a beautifully made plane," admired Friday. She couldn't help but appreciate the physics and geometry.

"Where's it going?" asked Melanie.

The plane kept gliding on and on, defying gravity with its pure aerodynamics. But then the wind slowly died, and the airplane began to glide down toward the polo field.

"I hope it doesn't hit anyone," said Melanie.

"It's only a paper airplane," said Friday.

"A *radioactive* paper airplane," said Melanie.

"True," conceded Friday.

In the distance they saw a horse canter onto the polo field.

"Oh no," said Friday.

The paper airplane was heading straight for the horse's bottom.

Friday cupped her hands about her mouth and called as loudly as she could, "Move your horse!"

The rider turned around. It was Princess Ingrid. She looked up and saw Friday. Melanie squealed and ducked down.

The paper airplane speared into the horse's backside, causing it to flinch with shock, then rear up.

Princess Ingrid was surprised, but you don't get to be the princess of Norway without knowing a thing or two about horsemanship. She crouched forward into the saddle, shortened the reins, and held on tight as the horse bolted straight across the field and plunged into the forest beyond.

"I think we've just caused an international incident," said Melanie.

"We didn't do anything," said Friday.

"No," said Melanie, "but when a valuable handwritten letter from the world's greatest female scientist gets ruined and an incredibly beautiful European princess gets carted off by an angry animal both at the same time, someone has to spend time in detention."

Friday sighed. She knew Melanie was right. "Let's go and see if we can salvage the letter."

The girls trudged out to the polo field and found the letter. It had been stomped into a big pile of horse manure.

"I don't think it will be worth as much on eBay now," said Friday as she pulled on gloves to protect herself from the radiation and gingerly picked the letter up by the one manure-free corner.

"That is the one! I want that girl arrested!"

Friday looked up to see the now very disheveled and extremely angry Princess Ingrid pointing at her from the great height of her horse. Her bodyguard was galloping over from the stables on a horse of his own.

"She is the one who attacked Maximus," said the princess.

"No, the paper airplane hit the horse's gluteus maximus," corrected Friday.

"Maximus is the horse's name," said the princess.

"You named your horse after a bottom?" asked Melanie.

"Detain her," yelled the princess. "Detain them both!"

"You and you must come with me," said the bodyguard, sliding off his horse. "We shall report to the Headmaster."

"And make sure he reports them to the police," said the princess. "They're probably anarchists or communists. They no doubt attacked me because they hate royalty."

"Well, I didn't before," said Melanie, "but I'm beginning to now."

The bodyguard grabbed them each by an elbow

and started leading them back up to the school. Ian Wainscott and the rest of the polo team trotted out onto the field.

"In trouble again, Barnes?" asked Ian.

It took some time to explain everything to the Headmaster, then to round up everyone who had touched the letter—the three boys, the librarian, and the horse—and arrange for them all to be decontaminated.

The letter itself would never be the same again.

"Are you upset to see an artifact by your hero get ruined?" asked Melanie.

"No," said Friday. "Given the sentiments of the letter, I think Marie Curie would have approved of having it stomped in horse manure. I bet she wished she'd thought of doing it herself before she'd sent it."

The Headmaster's parting instructions to Friday had been to stay away from Princess Ingrid.

"But she lives in the room next door to me!" protested Friday.

"I don't care how you do it," said the Headmaster. "You figure it out. It's bad enough with all the rampant criminal activity that goes on in this school, and hysterical students thinking there's some Pimpernel running loose. I don't want an international incident as well."

"It wasn't my fault the paper airplane hit her horse," argued Friday.

"You were involved in an incident that desecrated a historical artifact by a scientific heroine of Poland and France, while assaulting the buttocks of a horse being ridden by a Norwegian princess. There is barely a country in Europe you haven't rubbed the wrong way today."

"I try to be quiet and go unnoticed," said Friday. "That's the whole reason I wear brown cardigans—so I'll blend in."

"Whatever you're doing, it's not working," said the Headmaster. "So stop it."

"All right, if you say so," said Friday. "Although I do find it curious that when the plane hit the princess's horse, her bodyguard wasn't there. I wonder what he was up to in the stables."

"Well, I don't," said the Headmaster. "And if you know what's good for you, you'll keep your nose out of it as well."

Friday and Melanie were making their way back to their dorm room after a very nice dinner of chicken casserole. Neither girl had any intention of doing her homework. Friday was planning to spend the evening rereading *A Brief History of Time* and then writing Stephen Hawking a letter about all his errors. Melanie was planning to spend the evening napping so that she would be well rested for going to bed.

As Friday pushed open the door and flicked on the light she got

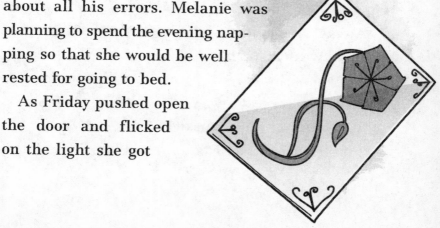

a nasty shock. There was someone sitting on her bed.

It was Ian.

"What are you doing here?" said Friday.

"Waiting for you," said Ian.

"Why did you break in?" asked Friday.

"I wasn't going to wait outside," said Ian. "Someone might see me. That's how rumors start."

"But everyone knows about you and Friday," said Melanie.

"Only in your mind, Melanie," said Ian.

"Why are you sitting in here waiting for me?" asked Friday, trying to get the conversation back on course.

Ian swung his feet off the bed. What he wanted to say apparently needed to be said with a degree of politeness.

"I was wondering if you would be willing to take tomorrow off from school?" said Ian.

"A date!" exclaimed Melanie. "At last! The tension was really exhausting."

"Not a date," said Ian. "I want . . ." He struggled to say the next word.

"What do you want?" asked Friday.

"I need some . . . assistance," said Ian.

"Assistance?" asked Friday. "With what?"

"It's a delicate matter," said Ian.

"Oh," said Melanie. "A personal medical issue?"

"No!" exclaimed Ian.

"Uh-huh," said Melanie. "I believe you."

"It's my mother," said Ian.

"Well, you shouldn't be telling us about her personal medical issues," said Melanie.

"No, my mother and father"—Ian swallowed and glanced at his feet—"are divorcing."

"I'm sorry," said Friday.

"Well, you should be," snapped Ian, "since you were the cause of it."

"I didn't make your father steal that diamond!" said Friday.

Ian shook his head. "I don't want to rehash all that. I need your help because my parents are separating and Mom doesn't have any money. Dad's hidden the assets."

"I can't help you with that sort of thing," said Friday. "You need a forensic accountant—someone who can trace bank transactions and track down offshore accounts."

"This is my father we're talking about," said Ian.

"He doesn't hide money that way. He converted all his cash into jewels: something physical that he really could hide. We know they're somewhere at our house, but we can't find them. We've looked everywhere— the freezer, the door panels, the secret safe in the floor of the panic room. Everywhere he normally stashes things. Mom even brought in a clairvoyant to see if she could sense the vibrations of where Dad had hidden them."

"So I'm the one you come to when the clairvoyant lets you down," said Friday.

"Look, I know you and I have a lot of baggage," said Ian, "but don't think about me. Do it for my mom. If

she doesn't find the money to pay the bills, she's going to lose our house."

"Why doesn't she get a job?" asked Melanie.

"She gave up law to be a circus acrobat," said Ian. "That doesn't look very good on your résumé."

"If my dad can hold down a job, anybody can," said Friday.

"Are you going to help or not?" asked Ian.

"Of course we'll help you and your mother," said Friday. "I am capable of human empathy."

"You are?" asked Ian.

"Even with someone as undeserving as you," said Friday.

"Mom doesn't have a car anymore," said Ian. "We'll have to take the bus."

"I'll call my uncle Bernie," said Friday. "He'll drive us to your house. He'll be good to have along. As an insurance investigator, he's used to finding hiding places."

As Ian got up to go to the door, something slid off Friday's bed. "You dropped something," Friday said, and bent to pick it up.

It was a plain business card. When she turned it over there was a picture of a blue-green flower.

"Is this yours?" Friday asked.

Ian looked genuinely confused. "No. It must have been on your bed when I sat down."

"What is it?" asked Melanie. "Is that a picture of a flower?"

"Yes, a particular type of flower," said Friday. "A pimpernel."

"This is getting exciting," said Melanie. "We've got our very own Aquamarine Pimpernel!"

"Is that what you call this color?" asked Friday. "I would've said blue."

"No, green," said Ian, looking over her shoulder.

"No, definitely aquamarine," said Melanie happily. "It's the calling card of the Aquamarine Pimpernel."

Chapter
10
The Wainscott Residence

The next morning at seven, before the residential adviser was awake enough to realize what they were up to, Friday, Melanie, and Ian snuck down to the front gates of the school, where they had arranged to meet Uncle Bernie.

"Why couldn't Uncle Bernie drive up to the top of the driveway and save us this walk?" asked Melanie.

"In case someone in the admin building was on the ball and activated the security gates," said Friday.

"The school has security gates?" asked Ian.

"They had to get them installed as part of the security arrangements for Princess Ingrid," said Friday. "Uncle Bernie could hardly ring the buzzer and ask to be allowed to drive up and abduct three students."

"It's not abduction if we agree to go," said Ian.

"No, it's just aiding and abetting truancy," agreed Friday. "Still, not a good look for Uncle Bernie. Whereas, if we're out on the street, that's another matter—he's just giving us a lift."

They reached the gates Friday was skinny enough to squeeze through between two railings, and Ian was athletic enough to climb over. Melanie was left standing on the wrong side.

"Go ahead. I'll have a nap and wait for you here," said Melanie.

"No you won't. You're coming with us," said Friday. "I'm not going to be stuck in a car with Ian and Uncle Bernie for the next two hours." She rifled in her bag and produced a battery-powered angle grinder and a pair of safety goggles. She put on the goggles. "Stand back!"

Two minutes and a lot of sparks later, Melanie was also on the far side of the now irreparably damaged fence.

In the distance a small car and a big plume of black smoke could be seen approaching.

"I'm assuming that beaten-up old brown sedan belching smog belongs to your relative," said Ian.

"Yes, that's Uncle Bernie," agreed Friday. "What he saves on buying a new car he spends on having to replace his oil once a week."

"Hi, Friday," called Uncle Bernie as he rolled down his window. "Where are we going?"

"Ian's house," said Friday. She turned to Ian. "Where exactly do you live?"

"Wellsdown," said Ian.

"Ooh, fancy," said Melanie. "Even among rich people, that's a fancy place to live."

"It's an expensive place to live when you've got no money," said Ian.

"Here, Friday, I got you a birthday present," said Uncle Bernie, handing Friday a box.

"But it's not my birthday," said Friday.

"Yes, it was. You turned twelve two weeks ago," said Uncle Bernie.

"You forgot your own birthday?" asked Ian.

"I've been busy," said Friday as she opened the gift and lifted out a new green porkpie hat. "Thanks, Uncle

Bernie, I love it." She leaned over and kissed him on the cheek.

"Let's get going, then," said Uncle Bernie, blushing.

"We'll have to make a stop along the way," said Ian as he climbed into the backseat.

"Where?" asked Friday. "Do you need to pick up some contraband? Electronics? Chocolate? Prewritten essays?"

"We need to swing by the butcher shop and pick up a big piece of steak," said Ian.

The reason for the steak became apparent when they pulled up outside Ian's house and a large, angry Rottweiler with a rhinestone-studded collar started barking and lunging at them from the other side of the fence.

"That's your dog?" asked Friday. "It's almost as friendly as you."

"That's Rocky. He's my father's dog," said Ian.

"Does he bark like that at your mother?" asked Friday.

"Yes, and there's nothing she can do about it," said Ian. "When you're negotiating a divorce settlement, it doesn't look good if you get rid of your husband's dog." He took the dripping red piece of steak out of the butcher's bag. "Here you go, boy." Ian hurled the meat over the fence to the far side of the garden. "Quick, make a dash for the front door."

The four of them hurried down the front path to the house. The yard had once been a nice ornamental garden before Rocky had been kept there.

The Wainscott residence was a large modern home. It didn't look too excessively fancy, but you could just tell that there was a tennis court and a pool tucked behind it somewhere.

Friday pressed the doorbell and they waited. They could hear Rocky savaging the steak on the far side of the garden.

"I wish your mother would hurry up," said Friday.

"I'm the shortest, so if that dog comes back my jugular is closest to its mouth level."

Ian reached across and pressed the doorbell again, three times in a row. But there was still no response. The sound of Rocky's snarling stopped; then they could hear his paws thudding across grass.

"Quick, run for the side gate!" urged Ian.

They all ran around the house. Rocky was racing toward them. Ian flung the gate open so Melanie and Uncle Bernie could race through. Friday was a few paces behind.

"Come on, Friday!" yelled Ian.

"She's not going to make it," wailed Melanie.

Friday leaped headlong at the open gate. Ian slammed

it shut behind her. She did a commando roll into a rosebush, and Rocky leaped up against the outside of the fence in futile protest.

"Wow!" said Ian. "That was . . ."

Friday struggled to her feet, then looked at the palm of her hand, where she had been pricked by a thorn. There was a drop of blood. She fainted.

"I was going to say impressive," said Ian, "but fainting kind of negates that."

Fortunately there was a water hose nearby, so Uncle Bernie was soon able to spray Friday in the face to revive her and they went in search of Mrs. Wainscott. As they walked around to the back garden, what they saw was a total surprise. Most houses in the neighborhood had immaculate gardens with pristine lawns and beautiful flower beds, all maintained by teams of well-paid gardeners. The Wainscott garden was nothing like that. It still had the rolling contours of a formally designed landscape, but every inch of it had been transformed into a market garden. Where once there had been lawn, there were now rows of every variety of vegetable. The tennis court had been planted with an orchard. The swimming pool was full of trout and water chestnuts. Amid it all roamed very self-entitled chickens helping themselves to snails and slugs from the vegetable garden.

"This isn't what I expected," said Friday.

"Money has been tight," said Ian. "Mother has taken up self-sufficiency. She grows all her own food."

"Sausage? Is that you?"

A woman who looked like an eighteenth-century peasant stood up in the middle of the cabbage patch. They hadn't noticed her before because her clothes were vegetable-colored and covered in dirt.

"Yes, Mom, it's me," said Ian.

"Your mother calls you 'Sausage'?" said Friday. "I'm so glad we came. This is better than being paid in money."

Mrs. Wainscott hurried over and wrapped Ian in a big hug. "How wonderful that you're here. You must see my eggplants—I'm going to have a bumper crop."

"Mom, I brought a friend from school," said Ian. "She's a detective and she's going to help look for Father's diamonds. Her uncle is an investigator. He's going to help, too."

"Hello, Mrs. Wainscott," said Uncle Bernie, holding out his hand. "It's a pleasure to meet you. You've got a fantastic crop of just about everything here. Your zucchini is amazing." He nodded toward a patch of lush, large-leafed plants.

"I know," said Mrs. Wainscott. "Growing things gives me such pleasure. I was a bad mother to my poor Sausage, always out at functions, wining and dining. But I hope in some way I can make up for all that by being a good mother to my veggies." Mrs. Wainscott looked fondly out at the expanse of her impressive vegetable garden.

"I don't think you can," said Melanie. Friday stood on her foot.

"Ow!" said Melanie.

"Shhh," said Friday.

"What?" asked Melanie. "No amount of homegrown tomatoes makes up for a neglected childhood."

"We're not here about that," said Friday. "We're here about the diamonds."

"Is it all right if Friday and Bernie take a look around?" asked Ian.

"Of course, dear," said Mrs. Wainscott. "But be careful of the lettuce patch. I put down fresh pig muck this morning, and it's smelling a bit ripe."

Friday and Uncle Bernie searched everywhere on the Wainscott property—all the places people think are secret but are actually commonly used by everyone else trying to hide things. They checked the freezer, the flour jar, the cavities in the tops of doors, the floors under the carpets, and the stuffing inside the sofa cushions. Uncle Bernie even used a radio-imaging detector he had borrowed from work to search all the walls and ceiling spaces. They found lots of stuff—$11.41 in loose change, Mrs. Wainscott's spare car keys, even a photo of Ian with a mullet haircut, which Friday regarded as priceless—but no diamonds.

"They've got to be here somewhere," said Friday. "Do you have any lollipops?"

"Why?" asked Ian. "Do you think Dad hid the diamonds inside candy?"

"No," said Friday. "Lollipops help me think. It's the calorie boost. The sugar stimulates cognitive activity."

"They've got ice cream," said Uncle Bernie. "I saw it when I was searching through the frozen peas."

So Ian, Friday, Uncle Bernie, and Melanie sat down and had a bowl of ice cream each while they considered the problem.

"It could be a purloined-letter scenario," said Friday.

"What's that?" asked Melanie.

"A literary reference to Edgar Allan Poe," said Uncle Bernie.

"It's a story about a man who hid a letter in a letter rack because it was so obvious that no one would think of looking there," said Friday.

"But where is somewhere so obvious you wouldn't think of looking for a diamond?" asked Melanie. "You don't have a diamond rack, do you?"

"No," said Ian.

"Maybe the chandelier," said Uncle Bernie. "You could hang the stones among the cut glass, and no one would notice them."

"That's a good idea," said Melanie.

"Except we don't have a chandelier," said Ian.

"We have to try to think like Mr. Wainscott," said Friday.

"You think you can mind-meld with a forty-nine-year-old convicted jewel thief?" asked Ian.

"Your father thinks he is cleverer than everyone else," said Friday.

"To be fair," said Ian, "most of the time he's right."

"He's also got a sense of humor and a flair for dramatic gestures," said Friday to herself now, muttering a series of thoughts. "The last I saw him he hid a massive diamond in his shoe. Now, where would he hide a series of small diamonds? People refer to diamonds as glass, but they also refer to them as rocks . . ."

Friday leaped to her feet.

"What is it?" said Ian.

"Rocky!" said Friday.

"Huh?" asked Ian.

"He hid his rocks with Rocky," said Friday. "The pun would have been impossible for him to resist!"

Chapter
11
The Savage Dog

Moments later they all had their faces pressed to the living room window, watching Rocky out in the garden. Rocky was mindlessly tearing apart an azalea bush.

"Look at his collar," said Friday. "Those aren't rhinestones. They're too sparkly. They're real diamonds."

"He put millions of dollars' worth of diamonds around his dog's neck?" said Uncle Bernie.

"It's brilliant," said Friday. "No one would think of looking there. If they went anywhere near

Rocky, he would savagely attack them. He is his own built-in security system. And if Mr. Wainscott ever escaped or was released from jail, he could come by and pick up his diamonds without even ringing the doorbell."

"That's just a theory," said Ian skeptically. "You won't know for sure until you have the collar in your hand, and how are you going to do that, smarty-pants?"

"I've never understood the origins of that expression," said Friday. "How can calling someone an 'intelligent item of clothing' be an insult?"

"You're getting off the point, Friday," said Uncle Bernie.

"It is a bit odd that your father would strap something so valuable to something so demented, stupid, and bloodthirsty," said Melanie.

"Rocky is brilliantly trained," said Ian. "Dad knows all about training animals from his time at Circus Skills University. But so that nobody else could order Rocky around, he trained him in Latvian."

"Why Latvian?" asked Friday.

"His childhood nanny was Latvian," said Ian. "Dad's fluent in the language."

"You speak lots of languages, Friday," said Melanie. "Is Latvian one of them?"

"No," said Friday. "I speak Russian. Surely it can't be too dissimilar."

"The gas-meter reader spoke Russian," said Ian. "He needed seventy-three stitches in his left calf. And he didn't get to read the meter."

"Who do we know who might speak Latvian?" asked Friday.

"Well, actually," said Uncle Bernie, "I do."

"Uncle Bernie!" exclaimed Friday. "You have a hidden depth."

"I was briefly a professional hockey player in the Latvian League," said Uncle Bernie.

"I didn't know that!" said Friday.

"You know how it upsets your mom and dad to hear sports talk," said Uncle Bernie. "I played for the Riga Raiders for half a season."

"What happened?" asked Friday.

"I got thrown out of the league for fighting on the ice," said Uncle Bernie.

"But I thought that's what hockey players do?" said Friday.

"Yeah, but I accidentally hit the lady who sang the national anthem," said Uncle Bernie.

"While she was singing the national anthem?" asked Melanie.

"No, she burst onto the ice with a bunch of spectators to try to punch our goalkeeper," said Uncle Bernie. "He'd just let in a home goal, so they were feeling emotional. Fists started flying, and my fist just happened to connect with her nose."

"Oh dear," said Friday.

"It was a mess," said Uncle Bernie. "They say her high notes never sounded the same again."

"Fascinating story," said Ian, "but, in summary, do you know the Latvian words for 'sit,' 'stay,' and 'stop biting my arm'?"

"I think so," said Uncle Bernie. "It has been a couple of decades since I've last tried my Latvian out. You don't often bump into Latvians. Especially not Latvians who don't speak better English than I speak Latvian."

"So long as your pronunciation is better than Rocky's, I'm sure you'll be all right," said Friday.

Two minutes later Uncle Bernie edged out the front door. As a precautionary measure, Ian had helped him duct-tape sofa cushions to his arms, legs, and head. As soon as Rocky sensed movement he spun around and ran full speed at Uncle Bernie.

"What do I say?!" Uncle Bernie asked in a panic.

"I don't know," said Friday from the safety of the other side of the screen door. "Try 'nice doggie.' "

"Jauks suns! Jauks suns!" yelled Uncle Bernie.

Rocky skidded to a halt.

"Awesome," said Ian. "This is actually going to work."

"Tell him to sit," advised Friday.

"Sédét!" yelled Uncle Bernie.

Rocky obediently placed his rear end on the grass.

"Now, slowly approach the dog and take the collar," said Friday.

"Do I have to?" asked Uncle Bernie.

"Yes!" said Friday and Ian in unison.

Uncle Bernie
slowly made
his way
toward
Rocky.
*"Lūdzu
nekož mani."*

"What's he
saying?" asked Melanie.

"Knowing Uncle Ber-
nie," said Friday,
"probably
something
like 'Please
don't bite
me.'"

"I hope your uncle isn't brutally mauled," said Mrs. Wainscott as she joined them at the door. "He seems like such a nice man. And he knows his veggies."

Uncle Bernie now had his hand on Rocky's collar.

"Labs suns, labs suns," he crooned.

Uncle Bernie unclipped the collar, patted Rocky, and started making his way back toward the house. "I've got it!" he yelled in English.

As soon as the English words were out of Uncle Bernie's mouth, Rocky snapped to attention, as if awoken from a trance, and launched himself at Uncle Bernie's bottom.

"Ow!" yelped Uncle Bernie.

"Don't worry, I'll save him!" yelled Mrs. Wainscott as she ran to the kitchen and grabbed a dozen slices of home-cured bacon. "Take that, you vicious dog!" Mrs. Wainscott hurled the bacon over Uncle Bernie. Rocky's head whipped up and he chased after the bacon, giving Ian and Friday a chance to drag Uncle Bernie inside.

"Did he hurt you?" asked Mrs. Wainscott.

"Only my pride," said Uncle Bernie.

"And your bottom," said Friday. "Look, you're bleeding."

"Never fear—I've been teaching myself how to sew," said Mrs. Wainscott. "I'll soon stitch that up."

"Maybe I should see a doctor," said Uncle Bernie.

"It wouldn't be worth the risk of walking past Rocky while you smelled of fresh blood," warned Mrs. Wainscott. "Don't worry, you'll soon be right as rain. Although you might not enjoy sitting down for a while." She went to get her first-aid kit.

Friday took out her jeweler's eyepiece and closely inspected the studs in Rocky's collar.

"Are they the real deal?" asked Ian.

"Please say they are," said Uncle Bernie. "I'd hate to be having the worst day of my life for nothing."

"They're diamonds, all right," said Friday. "Fifteen stones. All of them at least two carats. They're worth over fifty thousand dollars each."

"Seven hundred fifty thousand dollars!" exclaimed Mrs. Wainscott as she returned. "Why, that means that after we pay off the first and second mortgages, the car loan, the personal loans, the credit cards, and your father's dry-cleaning bill we'll be—"

"Rich?" asked Ian hopefully.

"Modestly comfortable," said Mrs. Wainscott. "If we mainly eat vegetables and the city council lets us keep using the pig-manure-powered gene-rator."

"So I don't have to quit school and get a job," said Ian.

"Which is a relief," said Friday, "because it's hard getting around those child labor laws. I know—I tried getting a job as a professional gambler once, and the police got surprisingly upset about it."

"That and the card counting," added Uncle Bernie.

"Yes," said Friday, "that, too."

"Thank you," said Ian.

"You're welcome," said Friday. "I know it's hard for you to say thank you because of your irrationally over-blown sense of pride."

"I wasn't talking to *you*," said Ian. "I was talking to your uncle. He's the one who got bitten on the back-side getting the diamonds away from the dog."

"Friday may have the brains," said Uncle Bernie, "but I've got the butt."

A Picture Is Worth
a Thousand Words

When they returned to school, things were different
between Friday and Ian. They weren't nice to each
other. They didn't even speak. But if Friday stumbled
and fell, dropping her books all over the hallway, Ian
no longer stopped to laugh. And if Ian put up his hand
and answered a question in class, Fri-
day no longer put up her hand and
corrected his grammar.

Without her feud with Ian,
school was almost relaxing. Friday
only had to worry about
avoiding her father. She
had a hard enough time

with the rest of the student body thinking she was a weirdo; she didn't want to be seen with her father and take on extra weirdness by association. So, to avoid walking past Dr. Barnes's classroom, Friday and Melanie took the long way around to get to English class, cutting through the ornamental garden, taking their shoes off, and wading through the fish pond.

"You've been getting on very well with Ian since you rescued his mother from poverty," observed Melanie.

"I know," agreed Friday. "It's nice, isn't it?"

"No, it isn't," said Melanie. "I had such high hopes for you two as a couple. If he's being nice to you, that can only mean one thing."

"He likes me?" guessed Friday.

"No, that he's in love with someone else," said Melanie.

"Who?" asked Friday. She was surprised.

"I don't know," said Melanie.

"Have you seen him being mean to someone else?" asked Friday.

"He'll never be mean to another girl the way he was with you," said Melanie. "That sort of thing only happens when there is true love, which only comes along once in a lifetime."

"Well, have you seen him being nice to another girl?" asked Friday.

"No," admitted Melanie. "But then, I haven't been paying attention. Plus he's really sneaky, so even if I were paying attention I might not notice. I bet he's the Pimpernel. He's elusive enough."

"Don't be silly," said Friday. "Next you'll be saying Debbie's the Pimpernel."

"She could be," said Melanie. "It would explain why she wears those glasses."

"She must wear them to improve her eyesight," said Friday.

"Barnes!" A seventh-grade boy hurried over to where the girls were sitting.

"My first name is Friday," said Friday.

"I know," said the boy. "But it feels weird to say it. I'm more used to it being a day of the week."

"What do you want?" asked Friday.

"The Headmaster sent me to get you," said the boy.

"But I haven't done anything," protested Friday.

"I think he's got a problem," said the boy. "When he was yelling at me to get you, his face was a very dark shade of reddish purple. My grandpa's face goes that color when he's really angry, or he's about to have a heart attack."

"Come on, then," Friday said to Melanie. "Let's see which it is."

"Oh, goodie," said Melanie. "I like being scolded by the Headmaster."

"You do?" asked Friday.

"The leather armchair in his office is so comfortable," said Melanie. "I start to drift off and don't hear a word he says once I'm sitting in it."

"Did you have anything to do with this!?" demanded the Headmaster.

Friday and Melanie's interview with the Headmaster was not as relaxed as they might have hoped. He was clearly incredibly angry and was waving around what appeared to be a gossip magazine.

"Hold it still," said Friday. "I can't see what you're flapping at us."

"Look, look!" he cried.

Friday took the magazine and studied the page the Headmaster was referring to. The headline on the page read "Secret Smooching at Swanky School" and had a grainy black-and-white photograph of Princess Ingrid kissing a boy.

"Who is that?" asked Friday.

"Princess Ingrid," yelled the Headmaster.

"I know it's her," said Friday. "I mean, who is the boy?"

"It's on the next page," said the Headmaster.

Friday turned the page, and there was a full-page blowup of the same photo that clearly revealed the boy Princess Ingrid was kissing.

"Ian!" exclaimed Friday.

"That rat!" said Melanie. "How dare he kiss another girl just because she is beautiful, rich, and royal!"

"I'm not here to discuss the inner workings of your adolescent love life," said the Headmaster. "I want to know how this happened."

"Well, when a boy and a girl like each other very much—" began Melanie.

"Not that!" yelled the Headmaster. "I want to know how. Electronics, especially cameras, are strictly banned. How did this photograph get taken and how did it get out to the magazine?"

"Hmm," said Friday as she stared at the photo. "It's surprising how low-tech a functioning camera can be.

All you need is a lightproof chamber and a tiny hole, then some photographic paper. It's just a question of capturing light."

"There's no way a member of the paparazzi has snuck onto the school grounds," said the Headmaster. "If the electronically monitored fence and security patrols weren't enough to deter them, then the law would. The courts are very severe with people who sneak into schools and take photographs of children without

permission. No photographer would risk it. They would do serious jail time. This was done by a student. I want to know who and how."

"So you want me to investigate?" asked Friday.

"No, I want to know—was it you?" asked the Headmaster.

"No!" protested Friday.

"Really?" said the Headmaster. "I know you've got a thing for this boy. If you admit it now, I won't expel you. I'll just make your life so miserable you'll wish you'd never been born."

"It wasn't me," said Friday.

"Do you have any idea how many times a day I hear those words?" asked the Headmaster.

"Why?" asked Friday. "Do you spend all day accusing students of crimes they didn't commit?"

The Headmaster slumped in his chair. He looked like he really wanted to expel Friday, if for no other reason than to cheer himself up. "All right, I do want you to investigate," said the Headmaster.

"What's the fee?" asked Friday.

"What do you mean 'fee'?" blustered the Headmaster. "Isn't it enough to be doing it for the good of the school?"

"No," said Friday. "I like this school, but I don't like it *that* much."

"Fine. Name your price," said the Headmaster.

Friday looked across at her friend. "I've already got my fees paid up to the end of next semester, so what do I want?"

"Kidney pie," said Melanie.

"I hate kidney pie," said Friday.

"Exactly," said Melanie. "We all do. Make him take it off the menu and you'll be a hero."

"Okay," said Friday. "I want kidney pie to be replaced with pepperoni pizza on Tuesdays."

"No anchovies," added Melanie.

"That's pepperoni pizza with no anchovies," stipulated Friday.

"Mrs. Marigold is not going to like that," said the Headmaster, referring to the Highcrest Academy cook. "You know how much she likes her kidneys."

"Those are my terms," said Friday.

"All right, deal," said the Headmaster.

A short while later Friday and Melanie were sitting on the bench in the rose garden outside the Headmaster's office, studying the magazine photo.

"The first thing we've got to figure out," said Friday, "is where the photo was taken."

"At the school," said Melanie.

"Yes, obviously," said Friday. "But where at the school? It's hard to work out because the photo is black-and-white and the background is fuzzy."

"Plus you're in love with Ian," said Melanie. "So you can't take your eyes off his lips."

"I am not in love with Ian," said Friday.

"Uh-huh," said Melanie. "And yet here you are, staring at a photo of him."

"I'm looking at the background!" said Friday.

"Of course you are," said Melanie. "Maybe you should look at his hair."

"I'm not obsessed with his hair," said Friday.

"No, I mean the angle of it," said Melanie. "It's strange."

"Maybe Ingrid ran her hand through his hair," said Friday. "That is something kissing people are known to do."

"How would you know?" asked Melanie.

"We didn't only have physics books in our house growing up," said Friday. "There was a small sociology section, too."

"Still," said Melanie, "his hair seems to be defying gravity."

Friday looked at Ian's hair. "You're right."

"I am?" said Melanie. "That's a nice change."

Friday tilted her head. "This photograph is at the wrong angle." She turned the magazine around. "They aren't standing up. They're horizontal."

"Ew," said Melanie, shielding her eyes. "Too much information."

"We need to talk to the victims," said Friday.

"My eyeballs?" asked Melanie.

"No, Ian and Ingrid," said Friday.

"You're not meant to go within fifty yards of Princess Ingrid," said Melanie.

"I know," said Friday. "I don't suppose she'd be happy about me standing fifty yards away and yelling my questions at her, either. I'll just have to talk to Ian first."

Friday and Melanie found Ian at the school stables rubbing down a polo pony. Debbie was there, too, cleaning tack.

"Doesn't the school have grooms to do that?" asked Friday. "I'd like to think our exorbitant fees go toward something constructive."

"They do," said Ian. "But grooming is an important part of building trust between a rider and his mount."

"You're both working as grooms for money, aren't you?" asked Friday.

Ian glared at Friday.

Debbie nodded happily. "That's right."

"If you tell anyone," said Ian, "I'll take your stupid porkpie hat and run it through Mrs. Marigold's food processor."

"Who would I tell?" asked Friday. "No one likes to be seen talking to me."

"Except me," said Melanie. "And if she told me, I'd probably forget."

"You already know, because you're here, too," said Friday.

"I suppose so," conceded Melanie. "But that's just a technicality."

"Anyway, I don't really care about your relationship with a horse and whether it's personal or professional," said Friday. "I'm here to investigate this photograph." She showed Ian the magazine.

Ian's face went bright red. "Who took that?!" he demanded.

"That's what I'm trying to find out," said Friday.

"Before the Headmaster has some sort of aneurysm."

"And why were you kissing her when we all know you're in love with Friday?" asked Melanie.

"That's not part of this investigation!" snapped Friday.

"So you admit you know it's true," said Melanie.

"I do not!" yelled Friday. "We are here to find out who took this photograph, and to do so we need to know where it was taken."

"The polo field," said Ian. "Right in the middle of it."

"Really?" said Melanie. "That's not very romantic or private. It's no wonder you got your photo taken if you were kissing there."

"We weren't kissing," said Ian.

Friday peered at the photograph. "What are you saying? That this picture has been digitally altered?"

"No," said Ian.

"Well, your lips are clearly pressed against hers," said Friday.

"And you are both lying down," said Melanie. "We can tell because of gravity and your floppy fringe."

"I didn't kiss Princess Ingrid," said Ian. "I was warming up my horse when she started yelling at someone on her cell phone."

"But students aren't allowed to have cell phones," said Friday.

"I don't think all the rules apply to visiting royalty," said Ian. "Anyway, her yelling in Norwegian spooked Butterfly Buttons."

"Who's Butterfly Buttons?" asked Friday.

"My horse," said Ian. "She reared. I fell off and landed on top of Princess Ingrid. She fell over and my face ended up pressed against her face."

"How embarrassing," said Melanie.

"Then her necklace got caught on my shirt button, so we were stuck to each other," continued Ian. "There would have been plenty of time for the photographer to set up the shot. Luckily, Ingrid had a pair of diamond-encrusted manicure scissors in her pocket, or we'd still be attached to each other."

"That story does not sound very believable," said Friday. "Are you just being chivalrous?"

"This isn't the seventeenth century," said Ian. "What interest would I have in being chivalrous? It would be more to my advantage if everyone thought I was the type of guy who made out with European royalty on a polo field."

"You're in luck," said Melanie, "because that's what everyone does think."

"I've got a hole in my best polo shirt that can prove it," said Ian. "Princess Ingrid sliced out a huge chunk getting her necklace free."

"I'll check out your shirt later," said Friday.

"I'm sure you will," said Melanie mischievously.

"But now let's go and investigate the scene of the crime," said Friday.

"I don't think you can call kissing a crime," said Melanie.

"The photograph," said Friday. "Taking the photograph is the crime."

"Oh yes, of course," said Melanie. "You're still pretending to be focused on that."

As Ian returned to grooming his horse, Friday stared at the back of his neck. The hairline was crooked. "Do you realize that there is a nick of hair shaved out of the back of your head?"

Ian rubbed the back of his neck with his fingertips. "I guess that's what happens when you have to go to a budget hairdresser."

"I'll cut your hair with the grooming shears next time," offered Debbie, with a giggle.

"So nothing was stolen from around your neck?" asked Friday.

"I did lose my room key yesterday," said Ian. "I kept it on a cord around my neck. Debbie suggested it. I assumed the strap snapped."

"Interesting," said Friday.

The Telltale Scale Model of Saturn

Look, there's the model of Saturn," said Friday as she held up the magazine and aligned the picture with her view of the school building. "So they must have been"—she took several paces to the right and a few back until the picture was perfectly lined up—"right about here."

Melanie looked at their feet. "Yes, this grass looks very similar to the grass they were lying on."

"So where was the person who took the photograph?" Friday turned and looked behind her.

There wasn't much to see on the polo field. It was just a large, flat area of grass. But along one side was a clump of bushes. "Over there!" Friday said.

The girls approached the bushes.

"Do you think a bush did it?" asked Melanie. "I've read *The Day of the Triffids*, so I know that plants are capable of much more wicked things than you might imagine."

"No, it must have been someone hiding in the bushes." Friday got down on her hands and knees and started crawling around underneath them.

"What are you looking for?" asked Melanie.

"I don't know," said Friday. "Some sort of trace evidence, I suppose."

"You mean like fibers or paint smears?" asked Melanie.

"Yes, that sort of thing," said Friday.

"So this sweater wouldn't interest you?" asked Melanie, holding up a top she'd found snagged on a branch.

Friday got up and looked in the collar. There was a name tag on the label. "Harriet Chow," she read out.

"I know her," said Melanie. "She's in ninth grade."

"If someone was crouched behind this bush, waiting for the perfect photo opportunity with the sun beating down, she probably would've gotten hot," said Friday. "Hot enough to feel the need to take her sweater off."

"You think Harriet did it?" said Melanie.

"Let's go and talk to her," said Friday.

When Friday knocked on Harriet Chow's door it was answered by a short girl with thick-framed glasses and the most beautiful glossy long black hair Friday had ever seen. It reached almost to the back of her knees.

"Harriet, I presume?" said Friday.

"That's right," said Harriet with a smile.

"Can we come in?" asked Friday.

"Why?" asked Harriet.

"We found your sweater in a bush," said Friday.

"And we think you sold a photo of Princess Ingrid kissing Ian Wainscott, so we want to search your room to see if you've got a camera," said Melanie.

Harriet laughed. "You can come in, but you won't find a camera."

Friday and Melanie stepped into the room.

Harriet smiled at them again.

"You seem awfully smug," observed Friday.

"Do I?" said Harriet, smiling even more smugly.

Friday looked around the room. Everything was as neat as a pin. It would be very hard to hide anything because all the school equipment and books were perfectly arranged so that everything was visible at a glance. Friday peered into the wastepaper basket. "May I empty this out on the floor?"

Harriet chuckled. "Of course, but only if you promise to pick it all up again."

Friday upended the bin. There was a lot of scrunched-up paper covered in notes and mathematical scrawl, several chewing gum wrappers, a warped piece of red cellophane, and two bottles of two-in-one shampoo. "Chewing gum is against the school rules," she pointed out.

"I know," said Harriet gleefully. "I'm a bad girl, aren't I?"

Friday started putting the rubbish back in the bin. "Ow!" She stopped suddenly and looked at her finger. A drop of blood started to form. Friday's face went white.

"Don't look at it!" urged Melanie. She rushed forward, pushing past Harriet, and covered Friday's finger with a tissue.

Friday sat down heavily on the floor. She breathed deeply and stared at the carpet while Melanie found a Band-Aid (she always carried them because she often fell over) and wrapped it around her finger.

"How did you do that?" asked Melanie.

"With this," said Friday, carefully leaning forward and plucking a sewing pin from the floor.

"Oh dear," said Harriet. "Sorry about that. But if you come into someone's room, empty out their waste bin, and search through their rubbish, what do you expect?"

Friday pulled herself to her feet. "May I look in your wardrobe?"

Harriet smiled. "If you like."

"You don't normally ask," said Melanie.

"I wanted to see how Harriet would react to the request," said Friday.

"And did I shock you?" said Harriet with a smirk.

"No," said Friday. "Your body language and facial expressions are entirely consistent with an overprivileged teenager who thinks she got away with something clever, and is therefore confident she will never be caught."

"Really?" said Harriet. "What a shame facial expressions can't be taken down and given as evidence in court."

Friday slid open the wardrobe door. It was as neat as the rest of Harriet's room. Her dresses and blouses were all hung up. Her sweaters and T-shirts were all folded and on shelves, and her shoes were neatly lined up on the floor. One pair was even still in the shoe box. Friday ran her fingers across the lid. There was a slight tear on the surface of the cardboard, as if someone had torn off a label.

Friday closed the wardrobe and turned to look around the rest of the room.

"Found anything yet?" said Harriet with a snigger.

"Yes. Melanie, you had better go and fetch the Headmaster," said Friday. "We've found our culprit."

The smug smile disappeared from Harriet's face. "You can't prove anything."

"Yes, I can," said Friday. "I've caught you red-handed with a camera."

"What?" said Melanie.

"I've found all the evidence," said Friday. "The red cellophane in the waste bin—"

"I was wrapping a present!" said Harriet.

"The cellophane is warped from exposure to heat," said Friday, "as it would've been when you wrapped it around a lightbulb to construct a makeshift dark-room in your wardrobe. Red light is used in darkrooms because it doesn't affect the photographic paper. Then there are the shampoo bottles."

"Washing my hair is not a crime," said Harriet.

"No, but according to any hairdresser, using two-in-one shampoo is." Friday picked up a bottle from the bin. "No wealthy student at this school would ever use shampoo-and-conditioner-in-one, certainly not a girl with luxuriously glossy hair like yours."

She opened the bottle and sniffed. "Just as I suspected—developing fluid." Friday opened the other bottle and sniffed that. "And this is fixative. So in this waste bin you have everything you need to make a darkroom to develop a photograph."

"But I don't have a camera," said Harriet.

"Yes, you do," said Friday. "I just saw it in your wardrobe." She strode over to the wardrobe and picked up the shoe box. "To make a camera, all you need is a lightproof chamber and a tiny aperture. This shoe box was your lightproof container. And the aperture would have been made by the pin

that I just pricked my finger on." She took the lid off the shoe box and held it up to the light. A tiny beam shone through.

"There's a pinprick in the lid," said Melanie.

"That is the aperture," said Friday. "The tear on the front is where Harriet would have taped a piece of cardboard across the hole to act as a shutter."

"You can't turn me in—I'll be expelled!" wailed Harriet. "And I can't get expelled. I'd be the first person in my family to get anything less than a postgraduate degree."

"I *can* turn you in," said Friday, "because that is what I've been hired to do, and I can't see any moral justification for what you've done. You only did it for the money. And your family must be well-off if you're studying here."

"But I do need the money," said Harriet.

"Why?" asked Friday.

"The Pimpernel stole my laptop!" wailed Harriet.

"I didn't see that coming," said Melanie.

"But laptops aren't allowed on school property," said Friday.

"I know," said Harriet. "That's why I couldn't report the theft. It was 3G-capable. I'd been using the laptop to do extra online study drills to keep my grades up. If my parents find out I've lost my laptop and my grades drop, they'll kill me."

"Surely they won't literally kill you," said Melanie.

"I don't want to find out," said Harriet.

"The first thing you need to worry about is not getting expelled," said Friday. "The Headmaster is seriously angry, but if you donate the proceeds from your crime to the school's beautification program, I'm sure he will be forgiving."

"But my laptop?" said Harriet.

"Don't worry," said Friday. "No thief is going to elude me for long. When I catch the Pimpernel, you'll get your laptop back, or at the very least get the ticket stub for the pawnshop he sold it to."

14

Trouble with Binky

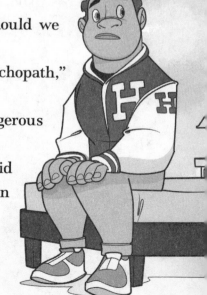

When Friday and Melanie returned to their dorm room, they found the door unlocked.

"Someone broke in," whispered Friday.

"Again?" said Melanie. "Should we go in and find out who it is?"

"It might be a dangerous psychopath," said Friday.

"Who at this school is a dangerous psychopath?" asked Melanie.

"Half the student body," said Friday. "And all the teachers in the math department."

"I suppose," agreed Melanie. "Well, we could stay out here, but the dangerous psychopath is bound to find us eventually, so we might as well go in and get it over with."

"All right," said Friday. "But stay behind me. If he's violent, I'll try reasoning with him while you run for help."

"I'd rather run to the dining room and have another pudding cup," said Melanie. "They were very good tonight."

Friday pushed open the door to the room. "Who's in there?" she called.

"It's only me."

Friday peeked around the door. "Binky?"

Melanie's older brother, Binky, was sitting on her bed. He was perched on the corner, because he was self-conscious about being a large boy and didn't want to rumple or break anything accidentally.

"Why did you break into our room?" Friday asked.

"I didn't," Binky said, shocked at the suggestion. "The door was wide open when I arrived."

"That's probably my fault," said Melanie. "Closing things isn't my strong suit. That's why I try to always leave the room with you. I know you'll close the door behind you. But if I'm on my own, the responsibility is too much."

"What are you doing here?" asked Friday. "Did you just come to visit Melanie?"

"No," said Binky earnestly. "I need help."

"You're not in a fight again, are you?" asked Friday.

"Gosh, no," said Binky, shaking his head. "Something much worse."

"What?" asked Melanie.

Binky leaned forward and whispered, "I've fallen in love."

"No," said Melanie.

"I know," said Binky, nodding his head in agreement.

"Know what?" asked Friday.

"Binky isn't very good at that type of thing," explained Melanie. "You know, expressing himself and talking to girls."

"He talks to me," said Friday.

"Yes, but I don't think of you as a girl," said Binky.

"Why not?" asked Friday.

"I think of you more as a figure of authority who rescues me when I get myself into trouble," said Binky truthfully.

"Well, that is nice," said Friday. "But you could think of me as a girl as well."

"I guess," said Binky. His brow wrinkled as he thought about it. "But it's not entirely my fault. You're the one who chooses to wear those cardigans."

"So who are you in love with?" asked Melanie.

"I don't know her name," said Binky.

"Why not?" asked Friday.

"Haven't had the courage to ask her," said Binky seriously. "She's too beautiful for just a run-of-the-mill sort of conversation. I'd have to think of something charming to say, and that could take hours."

"So where have you seen her?" asked Melanie.

"Here," said Binky.

"In our room?" asked Friday.

"She's your neighbor," said Binky.

"Ah, the princess," said Friday. "Everyone seems to be falling in love with her."

"No, not that one," said Binky, shaking his head. "She's not to my taste at all. She's too pretty and . . . princessy."

"I didn't know you had a type, Binky," said Melanie.

"I do," said Binky.

"So what does your love interest look like?" asked Friday.

"She's radiant," said Binky. His eyes glazed over as he imagined her. "She's petite, has shiny brownish hair, and has lips the color of, well . . . lips."

"So, in other words, she's short, has clean hair, and normal-colored lips," said Friday.

"Yes, that's her," said Binky happily. "And she has the warmest heart."

"How do you know if you've never spoken to her?" asked Melanie.

"Because she never says anything," said Binky. "She just glows through her eyes. At least, I think she does. It's hard to tell because she wears extremely thick glasses."

"You've fallen in love with Debbie!" exclaimed Friday.

"I have? She even has a pretty name," said Binky. "That's wonderful! I knew I was doing the right thing to come here. You always help me out."

"Why don't you just knock on the door and say hello?" said Friday.

"Are you out of your mind?!" said Binky. He looked horrified by the suggestion. "What would that lead to?"

"A conversation," said Friday.

"Well, that's not a good idea, then, is it?" said Binky. "Hardly my strength."

"He's got a point," agreed Melanie.

"Then what's your plan?" asked Friday.

"I was thinking of impressing her by running in the Potato Dash," said Binky.

"What's that?" asked Friday.

"Once a year they hold a race around the quad," said Melanie. "Runners have to sprint through the hallways of the buildings that make the four sides of the quad, then be the first to touch the flagpole in the center, all while carrying a fifty-pound sack of potatoes."

"It's a great honor to win," said Binky.

"The Vice Principal won it when he was a student here," said Melanie.

"Really?!" exclaimed Friday.

"There was a bout of chicken pox that year," explained Melanie. "He was the only entry."

"There is one flaw in your plan," said Friday.

"Only one?" said Binky in surprise. "What is it?"

"You're very slow," said Friday.

"That's a little harsh," said Binky, taken aback.

"I know my grades could improve, but I try my best."

"I don't mean your brain," said Friday.

"Although it is slow," added Melanie.

"I mean, you aren't very fast at running, are you?" said Friday.

"No, you do have a point there," agreed Binky frankly. "But you might have noticed that I am big. Obviously tall. But also, under these clothes—"

"Please don't be disgusting, Binky," said Melanie.

"I've got a lot of muscles," said Binky. "The football coach has had me lifting weights. I can bench-press a lot of those heavy disc things they put on the bar-bell. I thought if I got dressed in running shorts and a tank top, I might be an impressive sight. Catch the eye, if you know what I mean."

Friday shook her head to try and rid herself of the mental image of Binky in skimpy clothes. "I think I get the gist of it."

"So what do you need from us?" asked Melanie.

"I wanted to talk it through with you," said Binky. "Find out what you thought of it as an idea."

"It sounds like a terrible idea," said Friday. "But that doesn't mean it won't work."

The Potato Dash

W hat's that smell?" asked Melanie.

Friday and Melanie were standing with Binky at the starting line of the Potato Dash. All the other competitors were limbering up by stretching or by bouncing up and down on the spot.

Friday sniffed the air. There was a very disagreeable aroma. "It's part Tiger Balm, part fear sweat, and part chicken poo, which Mr. Pilcher, the groundskeeper, is currently watering into the flower beds on the far side of the science block," said Friday.

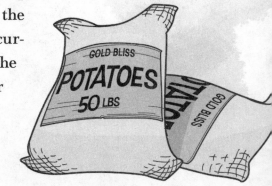

"I knew athletic events were unpleasant, but I didn't realize they would smell so bad," said Melanie.

"So who is the favorite to win?" asked Friday.

"Higgenbottom is fast, and so is Derrick Struthers, and Jamison," said Binky. "But Rajiv Patel and Derrick's brother, Jason, are devious. They're roommates. Last year they concocted a scheme to slow everyone down with banana peels."

"Did it work?" asked Friday.

"No," said Melanie. "The winner punched Rajiv in the nose and kept running."

"You're super brainy," said Binky, turning to Friday. "Do you have any tips on how to win a running race?"

"There's no point asking her now," said Melanie. "She's too distracted by seeing Ian in his super-short running shorts."

"I am not!" said Friday. "I haven't even noticed him."

Friday turned around and saw Ian right behind her. He was stretching his quadriceps while standing on one leg. Friday had never seen him in so little clothing before. Students usually wore polo shirts and much longer shorts for PE. Not that Friday ever attended PE lessons if she could avoid it. She'd never noticed how lean and muscular Ian's shoulders were before.

"Now she's too distracted," said Melanie.

"Wainscott is a double threat," said Binky. "He's fast *and* sneaky."

Ian smirked as he caught Friday staring at him. "Like what you see?" asked Ian.

"You have pleasing symmetry," said Friday truthfully.

Ian raised his eyebrows.

"You know you're good-looking, so you don't need me to tell you," said Friday.

Ian smiled. "Please stop flirting with me. I'm trying to concentrate on winning this race."

Friday's otherwise incredibly intelligent brain was suddenly unable to organize itself into finding a suitably cutting retort. All she could think to say was "Blurgh," but she realized this didn't sum up her thoughts and feelings adequately, so she simply turned back to Binky.

"Do I have to slap you to get you to focus?" asked Melanie.

"No, I'm focused," said Friday. "Run me through the rules of the race and maybe we can find a loophole."

"Oh, there aren't any," said Binky. "Cheating is traditional."

"You're allowed to cheat?" asked Friday.

"As long as you run from the starting line all the way to the finish line through all four buildings," said Binky, "it doesn't matter what you do to any of the other competitors along the way."

"That's appalling!" said Friday.

"Not at all," said Binky. "The headmaster who founded the race believed that cutthroat and brutally unfair competition was good preparation for real life."

"He's probably got a point there," conceded Friday.

"Do you have any thoughts on how you might cheat, Binky?" asked Melanie.

"Well, I am good at football," said Binky. "So I thought I could try tackling someone. Only problem is, it would leave me lying on the ground, too, and it's hard to win a race from that position."

"My advice is to run slowly," said Friday.

"Really?" said Binky. "I like the sound of that, because running slowly sounds easier than running quickly. But it's not the best way to win a race."

"You stand no chance of victory through cheating

or natural ability," continued Friday. "The only way you can win is if the whole race degenerates into total chaos and all the faster runners take each other out."

"That would be good," said Binky.

"All you've got to do is jog along at the back and try not to get knocked over," advised Friday.

"And be handsome while you do it," said Melanie. "To catch Debbie's eye."

But Binky had stopped paying attention. "Oh my gosh! There she is!"

Debbie was standing just a few feet away from them. They hadn't noticed her until now, because Debbie was the type of person you could easily not notice. She was wearing her usual baggy cardigan, but her hair was tied back in a ponytail and she was wearing runner's leggings.

"She's running in the race!" said Binky.

"Wow!" said Melanie. "Girls don't usually enter because it can get so violent and there are so many injuries."

"I didn't expect her to be the athletic type," said Binky.

"Is that a problem?" asked Melanie.

"Not at all," said Binky. "I'm prepared to be open-minded."

"Two minutes till we start," called the Vice Principal, who was acting as race marshal for the event. "Make sure you've all signed your legal waivers before the whistle goes off."

Debbie pulled her sweater off over her head.

"Gosh!" exclaimed Binky. "What a stunner!"

Friday looked closely at Debbie. She was wearing a very baggy gray T-shirt. Admittedly, with the leggings, she looked more athletic than Friday might have guessed. But Friday clearly wasn't seeing things through the same smitten haze that Binky was.

"Now you, Binky," said Melanie.

"What?" asked Binky.

"Take off your sweater," said Melanie. "That's the whole point, remember? You're supposed to be showing yourself off as eye candy."

"Oh, yes, of course," said Binky. He pulled his own sweater off over his head.

Binky had grown since Friday had first met him. He was at least six foot four now. And the weight work had paid off. He even had muscles in his neck. Friday knew she must have muscles in her own neck or else her head would fall off, but the muscles in Binky's neck were sinewy and purposeful like tree roots.

Friday noticed Debbie taking a secret glance at Binky's muscly chest. "Binky, I think you might be more brilliant than we realized," said Friday. "Your skimpy clothing idea just might work."

"Runners, lift your potatoes!" called the Vice Principal.

The entrants picked up their potato sacks. From the look of concentration on their faces, fifty pounds of potatoes balanced on the back of your neck was heavy just to hold, let alone run with. Friday and Melanie went to join the other spectators in the center of the quad, where they would be able to see all the action through the windows of each building.

"Remember, there are no rules. The first person to run through all four buildings and then touch the flagpole while still carrying his sack of potatoes is the winner. Is that clear?"

No one responded or even nodded their heads. They didn't want to dislodge their potato sacks from their necks.

"Take your places," called the Vice Principal.

All the entrants jockeyed for a good position on the starting line.

"May the superior entrant win!" yelled the Vice Principal before firing his starting pistol.

They were off, running at breakneck speed down the first hallway, shoving and bumping each other as they fought for the best position coming up to the first doorway.

Rajiv got there first and, in an act of blatant cheating, grabbed one of the doors and swung it back into Ian, knocking him down flat. This skittled half a dozen runners as they tripped over Ian, which caused the rest of the runners to bottleneck in the doorway, stumbling out and falling down the stairs. Binky, who was running at the back, leaped over the stack of fallen runners.

"Hey, you, that's not fair!" Binky called after Rajiv. Rajiv looked over his shoulder, as he stood at the top of the steps about to enter the second building and laughed. Binky, in an uncharacteristic flash of quick thinking, whipped off his size 14 shoe and threw it at Patel. It hit him neatly on the ankle, causing him to trip and slam into a vending machine.

The other runners swarmed past Binky, up into the

second building of the quad, and started sprinting. Binky was lumbering along at the back, wearing only one shoe. Debbie was in the middle of the pack. As they made their way into the third corridor, Derrick Struthers was now in the lead.

"It looks like Derrick is going to win," said Friday.

"You'd think so," said Melanie. "But something melodramatic always happens in this race."

Her words were immediately proved true. There was a tearing sound, and Derrick's potatoes spilled all over the floor. All the runners behind him started slipping and rolling on the potatoes, slamming into one another and tumbling down. Debbie stepped on a potato and her feet went out from under her, the potato sack around her neck pulling her over, and she landed facedown on top of three seventh-grade boys. Binky was the only runner left standing.

"Run, Binky!" yelled Friday.

"Run!" called Melanie.

But Binky stopped dead, dropped his potatoes, and bent over to help Debbie by picking up her sack for her. "These potatoes are very light," he said, confused.

Debbie blushed. "I hollowed them out," she confessed. "Have I shocked you?"

"I'm astounded," said Binky. "Not only are you beautiful, but you're brilliant as well."

"I'm going to use the potato centers to make mashed potatoes later," said Debbie. "Do you want to come over and help me eat them?"

"I'd love to," said Binky happily.

Binky put Debbie's sack back onto her shoulders, then swung his own sack into position. The pair started running, picking their way through the fallen runners and potatoes. Jason Struthers was up ahead and on his feet, at the front of the chaos. He burst out of the final doorway first and sprinted for the flagpole. Binky and Debbie chased after him. But Jason held his lead. He slapped the whitewashed timber, dropped his sack on the ground, and leaped in the air in triumph, accidentally kicking the Vice Principal with his muddy shoes, much to the delight of the crowd.

"Sorry about that, sir," said Jason.

"It's all right," said the Vice Principal, wincing. "As a fellow winner of the Potato Dash, I understand the ebullience that goes with victory—and in the record time of one minute and forty-nine seconds, too."

Princess Ingrid stepped forward with the winner's

cup and handed it to Jason. "Congratulations," she said formally.

Jason took the cup and grabbed Princess Ingrid in a big hug.

"Ew, gross!" she screamed, less formally. "You're all wet with sweat!"

Jason held the cup aloft and the crowd cheered.

"And now," said the Vice Principal, a smirk of pleasure returning to his face, "the traditional prize for the runner-up. A kick in the pants from the winner!"

Jason grinned. Binky stepped forward, resigned to his fate. The crowd whooped and hooted.

"Stop right there!" called Friday, stepping protectively in front of Binky. "No one will be kicking Binky in the pants today. At least, not for coming in second."

"Why ever not?" asked the Vice Principal. "I'll have you know this is an ancient tradition of the school."

"Hardly ancient," said Melanie. "The school is only seventy years old."

"Still, it is important to uphold customs," said the Vice Principal.

"Binky should not be kicked," said Friday, "because he did not come in second. He won, because Jason cheated!"

"What?!" exploded the Vice Principal.

"That's outrageous!" protested Jason. "I competed fair and square."

"Besides, cheating is allowed," said the Vice Principal. "It's in the rules."

"Oh yes, cheating is allowed," agreed Friday. "So there is nothing wrong with getting your roommate to slam a door on the rest of the runners. Or having your brother sabotage his sack of potatoes."

"You did those things?" asked the Vice Principal.

"Maybe," said Jason. "As you say, it is not against the rules."

"Exactly," agreed the Vice Principal. "That's just strategy and tactics. Entirely admirable."

"Unless they weren't tactics to slow down the other runners," said Friday. "They were tactics to distract everyone while one of the runners slipped out of the pack into a classroom, climbed out a window, ran counterclockwise around the outside of the quadrangle buildings, climbed in through another window in the science block, and rejoined the race, just as we were again distracted by all the runners falling over on potatoes."

"That's farcical," said the Vice Principal.

"Did you see Jason running in the second or third corridors?" asked Friday.

"Well, I'm sure he was there," said the Vice Principal.

"There were sixty runners," said Friday. "No one would notice if he slipped away when such dramatic accidents were occurring."

"You can't prove it," said Jason.

"That's where you're wrong," said Friday. "To prove you did exactly that, all I have to do is take one sniff of the Vice Principal's clothes." Friday leaned in and took a good long sniff of the mud stain on the Vice Principal's shirt front.

"Ew, gross!" exclaimed the crowd.

"Just as I suspected," said Friday. "Chicken poo."

"What?" said the Vice Principal.

"The race was run on linoleum flooring and asphalt," said Friday. "And yet Jason has muddy shoes, because he jumped out of a window and landed in a flower bed. And I know for a fact that only this morning Mr. Pilcher put chicken manure on all the flower beds on the east side of the school."

"Circumstantial evidence," said Jason. "My shoes could have gotten dirty anywhere."

"Then there was the hug you gave Princess Ingrid," said Friday. "According to her, you were disgustingly wet and sweaty."

"He was," said Princess Ingrid. "I'm going to have to get my entire outfit dry-cleaned."

"But that's impossible," said Friday. "The race only takes two minutes. But it takes the human body ten minutes from initial exertion for sweat to appear on the body and face. Look around you—even now, the other runners are panting but they are not sweaty. They will be in another three minutes."

"So I ran faster," said Jason, "and I started sweating faster, too."

"But I can prove the liquid on your face and body is not sweat," said Friday. She stepped forward and ran her finger down Jason's cheek then licked it.

"Ew!" chorused the crowd again.

"Just as I suspected," said Friday. "No salt. That liquid is not sweat—it's water from the sprinkler Mr. Pilcher set up in the rose garden. I bet right now there's a muddy footprint in your shoe size on the windowsill of the biology classroom."

"Cheating is allowed in the rules." Jason had a look on his face as if he would like to strangle Friday, but the race was over, so heedless violence would no longer be acceptable.

"Cheating is allowed," agreed Friday, "but to win, an entrant must run around the whole course."

The Vice Principal took the Potato Dash Cup from Jason, who seemed like he was about to burst into tears, and handed it to Princess Ingrid, who turned to Binky. She glared at him. "I'm going to present this to you, but that does not give you the right to hug me," she warned.

"Are you sure?" said Friday. "You're safe for another minute before he starts sweating."

"Quite sure," said Princess Ingrid, handing over the cup.

"I'll give you a hug," said Debbie, turning to Binky. "To thank you for your chivalrous behavior."

"All right," said Binky.

His head and neck turned bright red with embarrassment, but he bent over and gave Debbie a big bear hug. She smiled. Binky then clearly did not know what to do, because he gave Debbie a playful punch on the shoulder that nearly knocked her over.

"And now for the ceremonial kicking in the pants," said the Vice Principal. "You have to kick Debbie."

"Oh, I'd never dream of doing that," said Binky. "Can I kick Jason instead?"

"Just this once, I am prepared to bend the rules," said the Vice Principal.

Binky gave Jason a kick that would have made his football coach proud.

16

The Case of the Missing Microwave

When Friday and Melanie arrived at breakfast, everyone in the dining hall was watching Princess Ingrid be rude to Mrs. Marigold.

"This is ridiculous!" Princess Ingrid declared.

"What's going on?" Friday whispered to Ian, who was sitting by the door.

"Apparently, the princess doesn't like fish sticks," he said.

"I shall not eat this," continued Princess Ingrid in a loud voice. "I refuse to eat fish. They are nasty, smelly creatures that swim around in their own poo."

"They are a good source of protein and essential fatty acids," said Mrs. Marigold.

"They are slimy," denounced Princess Ingrid. "And I will not put one in my mouth." She dropped her tray with a clatter and regally strode from the dining hall.

"I've never seen a royal tantrum before," said Melanie. "I'm impressed."

"She's definitely got a flare for the dramatic," agreed Friday as they joined Debbie in the food line.

"Your roommate has impressive voice projection," said Melanie.

"She certainly does, but forget about that," said Debbie. "Did you hear about the lacrosse shed?"

"No," said Friday. "I didn't even know there was one."

"Well, it burned down last night," said Debbie. "Didn't you hear the sirens?"

"No, I was listening to Latvian language lessons," said Friday. "Just in case I come across any vicious Latvian-understanding dogs again."

"Well, there were lots of sirens," said Debbie. "First the fire engine came, then an ambulance, because one of the firemen had an allergic reaction to something in the shed and went into anaphylactic shock."

"You're very well informed," observed Friday.

"Oh, I overhead Mr. Rasmus the bodyguard briefing Princess Ingrid," explained Debbie.

"One of the benefits of having a royal roommate," said Melanie.

"It's just about the only one," grumbled Debbie.

It was Debbie's turn to be served. Mrs. Marigold gave her a generous portion of fish sticks.

The line shifted forward and Friday held out her tray. "Hello, Mrs. Marigold," she said brightly.

Mrs. Marigold scowled, scooped up the tiniest possible portion, and flicked it onto Friday's plate.

"Is that all there is?" asked Friday.

"It's all you're getting," said Mrs. Marigold. "Next!"

"But I'm hungry," protested Friday.

"You should have thought about that before," said Mrs. Marigold.

"Is this about the ban on kidney pie?" asked Friday.

"What have you got to do with the ban on kidney pie?" asked Mrs. Marigold.

"Nothing," lied Friday. "So what have I done to upset you?"

"You brought him here," said Mrs. Marigold, tears starting to well in her eyes.

"Oh, has my father said something to upset you?" asked Friday.

Mrs. Marigold sniffed and dabbed her eyes with the corner of her apron. "If only it was just that. I can take people talking nonsense to me all day long. I'm used to smart-aleck children and pompous teachers. But he broke my heart!"

"You're in love with my father?!" exclaimed Friday.

"Of course not!" retorted Mrs. Marigold. "Have you seen him lately? He needs a good hard scrub with a loofah and a proper haircut before any sane woman would look at him."

"Then what has he done?" asked Friday.

"He stole my microwave," said Mrs. Marigold. "It was a Sunbeam Pro 3000. I loved that microwave."

"That doesn't sound like Dr. Barnes," said Melanie. "He isn't exactly the stealing type."

"No, actually, it's just the sort of thing he would do," said Friday, "if he thought he could use it in an experiment. It would never occur to him to ask."

"Or perhaps he's the Pimpernel!" said Melanie.

"What?" said Friday.

"In the book, the Scarlet Pimpernel pretends to be a

bumbling fool so that no one will suspect him of thievery," said Melanie. "So maybe your father's socially incompetent, shambolic exterior is really just a brilliant disguise."

"Have you told the Headmaster about it?" asked Friday, turning to the cook.

"Never!" exclaimed Mrs. Marigold. "I'm not a tattletale."

"But you're prepared to take it out on my portion size, even though you've got no evidence or proof?" said Friday.

"If you can prove he didn't do it," said Mrs. Marigold, "I might consider allowing you to have full portions again."

"You can't withhold food from a child," argued Friday.

"You can have some of mine if you like," offered Debbie.

"If you give it to her, I'll take it back," threatened Mrs. Marigold. "Then there will be two hungry children."

Debbie looked horrified. "Sorry, Friday, I love fish sticks!" She scampered away with her breakfast.

"Are you going to report me to the Headmaster?" asked Mrs. Marigold.

Friday frowned.

"I thought not," said Mrs. Marigold. "Because if you complain about my portions, then I'll explain about my missing microwave, and you don't want the Headmaster to find out about that because then it would be your father in hot water."

"All right," said Friday, "I'll investigate. But I'm sure it's just a misunderstanding."

"A misunderstanding is when you accidentally pick up someone else's umbrella," said Mrs. Marigold. "It's not when you deliberately walk off with a microwave that isn't yours."

"I'll come and investigate the scene of the crime after breakfast," said Friday.

"Fine by me," said Mrs. Marigold. "But there's not much to see—just a space where a microwave used to be."

An hour and a half later, Friday was closely inspecting the kitchen bench with a magnifying glass while Mrs. Marigold sat with her feet up, sharpening her knives to ready them for the next day. Melanie kept the cook company, eating some leftover pudding (Friday was not offered any).

The industrial-sized dishwasher chugged away on the far side of the kitchen as Friday methodically searched. She prided herself on being able to find traces of evidence in any circumstance. But in this instance Mrs. Marigold kept her kitchen so spotlessly clean, there was no dust or dropped flour for Friday to find footprints in. There were no fingerprints either.

"Do you think the Pimpernel is a kleptomaniac?" asked Melanie.

"'Kleptomaniac' is just a fancy psychiatrist word for nasty thief," said Mrs. Marigold.

"It's a medical condition," said Friday.

"Being a low-down good-for-nothing is not a medical condition. It's a character flaw," said Mrs. Marigold. "I don't know why you're bothering to search here. It's your father's rooms you should be going through."

Mrs. Marigold looked at the blade she was sharpening. The edge evidently met with her satisfaction, because she tested it by running the knife along the back of her arm, shaving off some hair.

"Is that how you always test the sharpness of a knife?" asked Friday.

"Why?" asked Mrs. Marigold. "Is there something else you think I should be cutting?"

Friday decided it was best to change the subject. "What makes you suspect my dad?"

"Those loonies in the science department are always after my microwave," said Mrs. Marigold.

"They are?" asked Friday.

"Just last week, Mr. Davies wanted it," said Mrs. Marigold. "Said he needed to demonstrate crystallization to his seventh-grade class."

"Did you let him have it?" asked Friday.

"Of course not," said Mrs. Marigold. "I know what scientists are like. Always experimenting. It would start off with a crystal demonstration, and before you know it, he'd be making lava or microwaving dissected frogs."

"So why don't you suspect Mr. Davies?" asked Friday.

"Because Mr. Davies is comparatively normal," said Mrs. Marigold. "He has the good sense to be intimidated when I yell and threaten him with a soup ladle. He won't try messing with me again. Your father is a different kettle of fish."

"In what way?" asked Friday.

"He's always hanging around here," said Mrs. Marigold. "Complimenting me on my cooking and how lovely I look."

"Really?" asked Friday.

"He's not very good at it, mind you," continued Mrs. Marigold. "But he's always saying these awkward, flowery things, like 'Your raspberry cheesecake explodes with taste like a type-two star disintegrating in a supernova.'"

"That does sound like him," said Friday.

"And how my meat pie fills him with the—"

"Okay," interrupted Friday, "I think we've heard enough. I'll go talk to him."

"Yes, you do that," said Mrs. Marigold. "And get my microwave back while you're there."

"Just one more question," said Friday. "Has anything else gone missing recently?"

"No," said Mrs. Marigold. "Except . . ."

"What?" asked Friday.

"Well, I did lose an extra-large jar of peanut butter."

"I thought you weren't allowed to have peanut butter in the school in case a student is allergic," said Friday.

"I like it," said Mrs. Marigold. "I'm allowed to have

peanut butter on toast when I start work in the morning. I'm a grown-up."

"Perhaps that's why the Pimpernel stole it," said Melanie as she finished her bowl of pudding. "Because it's forbidden fruit."

"Have you found any calling cards with a picture of a blue flower on them?" asked Friday.

"*Aquamarine* flower," Melanie corrected her.

"Oh yes," said Mrs. Marigold, taking a handful of cards out of her pocket. "They're everywhere."

"Really?!" said Friday.

"The kids think it's so funny," said Mrs. Marigold. "They've made a whole bunch of them. If they want seconds of pudding, they put a card on their tray and say the Pimpernel stole their first serving."

"That would be the perfect cover for the real Pimpernel," said Melanie.

"Or perhaps your nutty father took the jar as well for some crazy reason of his own," said Mrs. Marigold.

"The Headmaster likes peanut butter," said Melanie. "Perhaps it was him."

"No, he could just confiscate it if he wanted some," said Friday. "Something strange is going on here."

17

Microwave Not Safe

Friday and Melanie went to confront Dr. Barnes. Friday had never visited her father's apartment before, because she had been avoiding him. He hadn't visited hers either, but that wasn't because he was avoiding his daughter—it just never would have occurred to him to visit her.

The teachers' accommodations weren't that different from the students' dorms, except that teachers got two small rooms, one for a study/sitting room and the other for

a bedroom, and unlike the students, the teachers didn't have to share, which was a good thing because teachers can be more childish than children when it comes to who gets the bed by the window.

Dr. Barnes was sitting at his desk, jotting down equations. He had run out of paper and was writing straight onto the desktop.

"Dad," said Friday.

"Hmm," said Dr. Barnes, not even looking up.

"Did you steal Mrs. Marigold's microwave?" asked Friday.

"Whatever you want to do is fine with me," replied Dr. Barnes.

"I don't think he's listening," said Melanie.

Dr. Barnes glanced up. "Do you need me to sign a permission slip or something?"

"No, I need you to tell me whether or not you stole Mrs. Marigold's microwave," said Friday.

"Mrs. who?" asked Dr. Barnes.

"Marigold," said Friday. "The school cook. She says you hang around her kitchen all the time."

"Oh yes," said Dr. Barnes.

"Are you in love with her?" asked Melanie.

"Yes," said Dr. Barnes.

"You are?!" exclaimed Friday.

"Her desserts are extremely good," said Dr. Barnes. "Her practical application of the principals of carbon chemistry and thermal dynamics, as it pertains to foodstuffs, is truly impressive."

"But what about Mom?" asked Friday.

"Her?" said Dr. Barnes. "She can't cook at all."

"But you're still married," said Friday.

"So?" said Dr. Barnes. "I'm allowed to eat another woman's puddings."

"But you just said you were in love with her," said Friday.

"Did I?" said Dr. Barnes. "Well, it only makes sense. Food consumption is a more rational basis for affection than most."

"Then why did you steal her microwave?" asked Friday.

"Her microwave?" said Dr. Barnes. "But a microwave is regular fluctuation in the light spectrum. I didn't know the technology existed to steal one."

"A microwave is also a kitchen appliance," said Friday.

"Really?" said Dr. Barnes. "How extraordinary!"

"Did you steal an appliance from Mrs. Marigold's kitchen?" demanded Friday.

"I don't think so," said Dr. Barnes. "But it is impossible to prove a negative."

"I'm going to search your rooms," said Friday.

"Go ahead," said Dr. Barnes. "Can I get back to my equations now?"

"Sure," said Friday.

She and Melanie searched the apartment. It only took one minute. Dr. Barnes had very little stuff, and there were few places in the small rooms that you could hide anything as large as a microwave.

"Did you steal it and hide it anywhere else?" asked Friday, going back to where her father was working.

"What?" asked Dr. Barnes.

"I don't think there's any point asking him," said Melanie. "He doesn't seem to know much about anything."

"I'll have you know I'm one of the world's leading thinkers on M-theory," said Dr. Barnes.

"Exactly," said Melanie. "He doesn't know much."

"So if Dad didn't do it," said Friday as she and Melanie walked back across the quad, "who else could have a possible motive for stealing a microwave and a huge jar of peanut butter?"

"Someone who likes hot peanut butter sandwiches?" said Melanie.

"Microwaving doesn't improve bread," said Friday.

A boy ran over to them. "The Headmaster wants to see you in the supply closet," said the boy, panting to regain his breath.

"That sounds ominous," said Friday.

"Maybe he's just tired of yelling at you in his office," said Melanie. "And he wants to branch out and try doing it somewhere else."

When Friday and Melanie found the Headmaster he was standing amid a pile of splintered wood.

"Look!" exclaimed the Headmaster. "Do you know anything about this?"

"I don't think so," said Friday, crouching down to get a closer look at the wood splinters.

"What do you mean?" demanded the Headmaster. "Either you know or you don't."

Friday picked up a splinter. It was raw wood on one side and had red and black stripes on the other. "They're pencils," said Friday.

"I'm glad I called for you," said the Headmaster

sarcastically. "Thank goodness I have my own Sherlock Holmes on hand to tell me the extremely obvious."

"But without the lead," continued Friday. She sifted through the pile of splinters. "Someone has destroyed these pencils and taken all the lead."

"Yes, weird isn't it?" said the Headmaster. "That's why I sent for you. Weird seems to be your area of expertise. So do you have any idea why we have a lead thief on our hands?"

"Pencil lead doesn't actually contain lead," said Friday. "It's made of graphite."

"Thank you for the lesson on pedantic detail," said the Headmaster. "I can understand someone stealing my watch, or Jacinta Holbrooke's earrings last week, or Bruce Viswanathan's collection of Hemingway first editions yesterday, but can you please explain to me why on earth anyone would want to steal the graphite out of a pencil?"

"Because they're the elusive Pimpernel?" suggested Melanie.

"No, I know exactly why," said Friday. "Because they're an idiot with a get-rich-quick scheme."

"And where shall we find this idiot?" asked the Headmaster.

"Mr. Davies's sixth-grade science class," said Friday, checking her watch. "Their lesson should start in five minutes."

When Friday burst into Mr. Davies's classroom six minutes later, with Melanie and the Headmaster in her wake, Mr. Davies was in the middle of an explanation of why water expands when it freezes.

"Aha!" cried Friday. "You're still teaching crystallization, I see!"

"It's in the curriculum," said Mr. Davies. "I'd get in trouble if I didn't."

"And so all the facts fall into place," said Friday. "We know what was stolen, and now I know why."

"*Why* is all very well," said the Headmaster, glaring at the class, "but I'd like to know *who*."

"All we need to do is find out which of these students has damaged cuticles," said Friday.

Mirabella Peterson hastily sat on her hands.

"You! Mirabella! You are hiding evidence under your bottom," accused Friday.

"You can't search me without a search warrant!" declared Mirabella.

"We don't want to search you, we just want to see your fingers," said Friday.

"I'm not moving," said Mirabella defiantly.

The Headmaster sighed. "You know, there are some days when I hate dealing with children."

"I thought that was every day," said Melanie.

"Am I going to be allowed to continue my lesson?" asked Mr. Davies.

"That depends on how long it takes us to locate the microwave Mirabella stole," said Friday.

"You'll never find it!" cried Mirabella. "I mean, it wasn't me—you can't prove anything!" she corrected herself hastily.

"Could you just explain your theory," the Headmaster asked Friday, "so that I can decide whether to suspend Mirabella for being a thief or you for wasting my time?"

"Mr. Davies has been teaching his class about crystallization," explained Friday. "Diamonds are crystals. Given Mirabella's character—"

"She's superficial and mean," said Melanie.

"Exactly," agreed Friday. "I doubt she has much interest in science, generally. But talk of diamonds would have caught her attention. Did you by any chance discuss how diamonds can be manmade?"

"Yes, we did," said Mr. Davies.

Friday nodded. "And one of the ways you can synthesize a diamond is ultrasonic cavitation."

"That's right," agreed Mr. Davies. "It's the latest experimental method."

"To create a diamond with ultrasonic cavitation, you need a source of carbon and a carbon seed crystal. Then you bombard them with microwaves," said Friday.

"Like Mrs. Marigold's missing microwave?" said Melanie.

"Precisely," said Friday. "Once you have a microwave plus peanut butter, which is a source of carbon, and graphite, which is a form of crystallized carbon, you have all the ingredients to make your own diamonds."

"You do?" asked the Headmaster.

"Or rather, you *think* you do," said Friday. "If you don't realize that you can't achieve the right kind of microwaves with a domestic kitchen appliance, you don't realize that pencil graphite includes large amounts of impurities, and you're deluded enough to believe peanut butter could ever be transformed into a clear quality diamond."

"But he said it was possible," accused Mirabella,

pointing at Mr. Davies and revealing her scraped and bloodied fingertips. "All I got was a sticky mess of burned charcoal!"

"Where is the microwave now?" demanded Friday.

Mirabella looked sheepish. "You know how the lacrosse shed burned down last night . . . and how one of the firemen got an allergic reaction . . . ?"

"Yes," said the Headmaster quietly. He didn't want to frighten Mirabella with his welling rage before she made a full confession.

"Well, I've got a key to the shed because I'm captain of the under-thirteens' lacrosse team," said Mirabella. "So I put the jar of peanut butter in the microwave with the pencil lead jammed in the middle, then set the microwave on high for six hours. When I got back the shed was on fire."

"That was you?" said Mr. Davies.

"I wasn't worried, because I knew diamonds could withstand extreme heat," said Mirabella, "but after Mr. Pilcher put the fire out, the fireman recovered from his anaphylactic shock, and everyone left, I looked through the charcoal remains and found the shell of the microwave. When I looked inside, there were no diamonds, just burned, sticky peanut butter."

"But ultrasonic cavitation only produces industrial diamonds," said Mr. Davies.

"That's what I wanted," said Mirabella. "An industrial-sized diamond."

"No, industrial diamonds are microscopic gray diamond dust," said Friday. "They're used for making sandpaper, not jewelry."

"You mean," said Mirabella, horrified, "I damaged my cuticles for nothing?!"

"I'm afraid so," said Friday.

"Pooh, I knew I should have dropped science and taken geography instead," said Mirabella. "At least with Mr. Maclean you can cheat and he'll never notice."

"Mrs. Marigold is going to be upset that she's not getting her microwave back," said Melanie.

"At least it wasn't Dad," said Friday.

"Or the Pimpernel," said Melanie.

"Unless Mirabella is the Pimpernel," said Friday.

They both looked at Mirabella. Her bottom lip was stuck out in a pout as she inspected her damaged cuticles.

There clearly wasn't a trace of remorse in her brain for destroying the lacrosse shed or nearly killing a firefighter.

"No," said Friday. "She's too convincing as a dimwit. There's no way she could be faking it."

The Case of the Voice in the Night

Friday, I want to hire your services," said Pauline Yu.

Friday and Melanie were sitting in the quietest corner of the common room, where all the nerds liked to sit. Friday was doing her homework and Melanie was taking a nap, facedown, on her homework. A notebook could be very comfortable.

Friday had never spoken to Pauline before. Not that Pauline was unfriendly; she just didn't speak much. She was usually working. She was the top math student in tenth grade. In sophomore year, the top students got

to study calculus. Friday looked forward to the day when she could move on from algebra and dive into the deep end of calculus. She already thoroughly understood the subject better than most professors of mathematics. But it was more fun than algebra because you got to spend a lot of time drawing graphs.

"What's the problem?" asked Friday.

"There's someone in terrible trouble," said Pauline.

"Who?" asked Friday.

"I don't know," said Pauline.

"Then how do you know they're in terrible trouble?" asked Friday.

"Because I hear them calling for help," said Pauline.

"Okay," said Friday. "We're going to have to swap to narrative discourse. The Socratic method is clearly not telling me what I need to know here."

"Excuse me?" said Pauline. "I'm a math genius. I don't understand your linguistic references."

"Tell me your story, then," said Friday. "My questions aren't helping me understand."

"The last three nights I've been woken up by a voice," said Pauline.

"In your head?" asked Melanie, stirring from her nap. "I hate it when they get noisy."

"No, in the roof," said Pauline.

"Okay, that's even stranger," said Friday. "Are you sure it's not just a possum or a rat? People often tell themselves the noise on their roof is a possum, but that's only because they don't want to think it's a large rat."

"No, it's a person," said Pauline. "The voice speaks to me clearly. It says, 'Help me, help me, I'm in the attic.' "

"That's very specific," said Friday.

"The voices in my head usually just tell me to get up and go to the bathroom," said Melanie.

"So what did you do?" asked Friday.

"I tried to help them, of course," said Pauline.

"That's very kind of you," said Melanie.

"Kindness has nothing to do with it," said Pauline. "I need my rest if I'm going to function efficiently. Complying with the request is the most logical way to get the voice to shut up."

"Did you call for the dorm adviser?" asked Friday.

"No, she's not nice," said Pauline. "If you disturb her between the hours of eight p.m. and eight a.m., she makes you do fifty push-ups."

"I would have tried earplugs," said Melanie.

"You wouldn't have woken up for some voice in the first place," said Friday.

"True," agreed Melanie. "Not unless it was accompanied by a bucket of water and flashing bright lights."

"So we went to investigate." Pauline turned and beckoned to her roommate, Sienna Moorcroft, who joined them. "Sienna has a flashlight. We went down the hallway to the attic stairs, climbed up, and took a look."

"What did you find?" asked Friday.

"Did your dorm adviser lock someone on the roof?" asked Melanie.

"No," said Pauline. "We found absolutely nothing."

"Then what did you do?" asked Friday.

"We went back down to our room and went back to sleep," said Pauline.

"And the voice had stopped?" asked Friday.

"Yes, there was no more noise from the attic," said Pauline. "Until last night, when it started again."

"What did it say?" asked Friday.

"The same thing, 'Help me, help me, I'm in the attic,'" said Pauline. "But again, when we went upstairs there was nothing to see."

"Except for lots of gross cobwebs," added Sienna. "And stinky mold."

"Intriguing," said Friday. "Melanie, we are going to have a nocturnal escapade."

"Oh dear," said Melanie. "This is going to involve me getting less than my usual eight hours of sleep, isn't it?"

"I doubt it," said Friday, "since you manage to nap up to four hours a day. You could spend an hour investigating the attic with me and still be ahead by three hours."

Chapter
19
Sleuthing Sleepover

That night, Friday and Melanie bedded down on Pauline and Sienna's floor. They didn't own sleeping bags, because they were concerned that type of thing might lead to being forced to go camping, so they simply lay on the carpet with their quilts and pillows. Once they moved the floor lamp over by the desk and Pauline's extensive collection of math textbooks into the closet, there was plenty of room. Melanie, of course, went straight to sleep. Friday's brain always took a little longer to wind down. She was 892 digits into reciting pi before her brain finally clocked off.

Friday was having a delightful dream in which the truth about the universal theory of space and time was about to be revealed to her when she heard a boy's voice saying, "Help me, help me!" At first Friday's brain thought it was a theoretical physicist asking for advice on an equation, but then her brain rejected that thesis when it realized that this was the voice in the attic.

"Help me, please! I'm in the attic," wailed the voice.

"Melanie! Did you hear that?" asked Friday.

Melanie had not. She was deeply submerged in sleep. But Pauline and Sienna were awake. They had their flashlights ready and were getting out of bed. Friday put on her own night-vision goggles (a gift from a Navy SEAL whom she'd tutored in trigonometry— there is a surprising amount of trigonometry in being a sniper).

"Melanie, wake up!" said Friday, shaking her friend.

"There's no time," said Pauline, grabbing Friday by the arm. "We've got to help him."

The three girls ran down the hallway. "The attic stairs are this way," said Sienna.

"What if the door is locked?" asked Friday.

"Not a problem," said Sienna. "I stuck a whole pack

of chewed chewing gum in there so that no one could lock it."

"Chewing gum is against the school rules," said Friday.

"You can't prove it was mine," said Sienna. "It's in the lock, not in my mouth."

"What if the Headmaster had the chewing gum DNA-tested?" asked Friday.

"Princess Ingrid would be in a lot of trouble, then," said Sienna.

"What?" said Friday.

"I didn't say I was the one who had chewed the gum," said Sienna.

The girls burst through the door and ran up the attic stairs. Friday was panting hard. This was the farthest she had run since the PE lesson in which the teacher turned her back and Friday dashed to the locker rooms to hide.

They could still hear the voice. "Help me, help me!" it cried.

Finally they reached the top of the stairs. The attic was a large cavernous room, like a huge triangular tube. They could stand easily in the middle, but the roof sloped down to the sides of the building. There was no proper flooring underfoot. The timber frame had been filled in with insulation mats.

"Be careful," said Sienna. "You've got to step on the beams. The insulation is only supported by the plaster ceiling below."

"Your foot will go right through," added Pauline.

"So where is your room?" asked Friday.

The voice had fallen silent.

"About halfway down on the right," said Pauline.

The girls started carefully leaping from beam to beam to get to the spot directly above their dorm room. The attic was very dark, and there were cobwebs and mysterious droppings everywhere. Friday was not a superstitious person, but everything about this big, empty, uncomfortable room was creepy. Her senses were screaming at her to go back. "This is the spot," said Pauline, stopping on a beam about halfway down. "I marked where our room was with a piece of chalk." She shone her flashlight on the beam. An "E" was marked in white chalk.

"Pauline," said Friday, "I don't suppose there's any chance that you sleepwalk and go around marking things with chalk when you're fast asleep?"

"No, why?" asked Pauline.

"Take a look at the other beams," said Friday.

Pauline raised her flashlight to scan the long row of beams along the rest of the attic.

"Aaaggghh!" screamed Pauline and Sienna.

Identical "E"s had been written on the same spot on every beam in the room.

"It's a ghost!" exclaimed Sienna.

"I'm being punished for taking glucose tablets as a study aid!" wept Pauline.

"Get a grip!" said Friday. "I don't for a moment believe that slapping is a medically sound treatment for hysteria. But I'm prepared to try it, because I can see that slapping would be of therapeutic benefit to the person having to endure listening to hysteria."

Pauline and Sienna calmed down a little bit.

"Just because we are standing in an unpleasant-smelling attic, in the dark, in the middle of the night, surrounded by spiderwebs, animal droppings, and goodness knows how many rodents, that does not mean that the rules of common sense no longer apply," said Friday. "We are perfectly safe here."

Unfortunately Friday emphasized her point by stomping her foot. She missed the beam and her foot slid down the side of an insulation mat and punched through the plaster underneath.

"Aaagghh!" cried Friday as she fell, her leg disappearing through the floor into the room below.

"Aaagghhh!" screamed Pauline and Sienna, who despite Friday's stirring speech were perfectly prepared to believe that a ghost had chopped Friday's leg off.

"Ow!" said a voice from below. It was Melanie. "Friday, is that you? I can't imagine there would be two students at this school wearing periodic table pajama pants."

"Yes, it's me," said Friday, struggling to pull her leg back up into the attic.

"Why is your leg dangling from the ceiling?" Melanie asked, her voice muffled by the plaster and insulation between them. "And why did you stomp a piece of plaster ceiling onto my head."

"Sorry," said Friday. "It was an accident. We're in the attic investigating the voices."

"Is it you, then?" asked Melanie.

"What?" asked Friday.

"Well, you're in the attic," reasoned Melanie. "And I can hear your voice."

"No . . . ugh." Friday finally managed to pull her leg back up. She turned around and crouched down so she could see Melanie through the rather large hole her leg had created. "We're investigating the other voice. The one that's been calling, 'Help me, help me.' Sorry about the plaster."

It was pretty dark down in Pauline and Sienna's room, but Friday could still see the large pieces of plaster scattered all over Melanie, and Sienna's reading lamp had been knocked over onto her, too. Melanie didn't like being woken up at the best of times, but to be woken up like this would be unpleasant for anybody.

"That's all right," said Melanie. "It doesn't hurt too much. I think my nose broke its fall."

"I've got one more thing to search for up here," said Friday. "Then we'll be down." She turned to Pauline and Sienna. "Well, I know what happened. It's just a question of finding the evidence and confronting the guilty party." Friday crouched down again and started pulling up one insulation mat after another and looking underneath.

"What are you looking for?" asked Pauline.

"Aha!" Friday pulled a small black box out from under a wad of insulation.

"What is it?" asked Pauline.

"A wireless speaker," said Friday. "Someone has been using this to broadcast cries of help directly above your dorm room."

"Why would anyone want to do that?" asked Pauline. "Were they planning to lure us up here and lock us in the attic as some kind of prank?" asked Sienna.

"No," said Friday. "Their motives were the precise reverse. It's not that they wanted you up here. It's because they wanted you out of your room."

"Why?" asked Pauline.

"Think about it," said Friday. "What motive would someone have for breaking into your room specifically?"

"I don't know," said Pauline.

"That's the problem with working so hard to be a math genius but not focusing on your lateral thinking," said Friday, shaking her head. "It's because you are the best math student in your grade."

"In the whole school," said Pauline.

"I wouldn't go that far," said Friday. "I'm only in sixth grade. I haven't had the opportunity to flex my mathematical muscles yet. But I digress. In your room each night sits one object of particular value—your answers to your math homework. They would be tempting to a less able student ambitious for higher grades."

"So they came up with this crazy scheme to get us up in the attic?" said Pauline. "That's just silly."

"It's ingenious," said Friday. "As soon as they saw you disappear up the staircase they could enter your room. You left your door unlocked because you're wearing your pajamas, and it's dark so you didn't want to take your key. While they're in your room searching for your homework, they can hear your footsteps on the beams above so they would know exactly where you were and when you were returning, so they had time to make their escape."

"It still sounds crazy," said Pauline.

"But we have further evidence," said Friday. "Your reading lamp. When I looked down through the hole, it was lying across Melanie. When we left your room, the lamp was over by the desk. So the plaster from the roof couldn't have made it fall. A person must have knocked it over in panic, when my leg smashed through the ceiling."

"Wouldn't Melanie have noticed if there was someone creeping about the room?" asked Sienna.

"I doubt it," said Friday. "I once accidentally generated a sonic boom in our dorm room while Melanie was napping, and she didn't notice that. So I doubt she would notice a person trying to be quiet. Come on, let's check out your room."

When they got back down to the
dorm room Friday didn't let Pauline
and Sienna enter right away. She didn't let Melanie
move, either. This suited Melanie. She used the opportunity to go back to sleep. Friday closely inspected
the dust debris from the plaster collapse.

"What can plaster dust tell you about someone
stealing my homework?" asked Pauline.

"It tells me that there was one intruder," said Friday.
"He was a boy with size twelve feet. From the length
of his strides, I'd say he was about six foot two."

"Can you really see footprints?" asked Pauline. "It
just looks like dust to me."

"Yes, his sweaty feet picked up the dust as he ran out of the room," said Friday. "You can see he was standing by the desk when the roof partially collapsed, because his aerial outline has been stenciled in dust."

"That just looks like a less dusty patch on the carpet," said Sienna.

"And that's exactly what it is," said Friday. "Let's see what he was looking at."

The three girls walked across the debris to the desk. Pauline's math homework was lying faceup in the center. It consisted of three sheets of paper covered in equations.

"Is this the way you left your work?" asked Friday.

"No," said Pauline. "It was put away in my homework folder."

"He can't have been photographing your homework," said Friday. "Thanks to Princess Ingrid, the Headmaster has been extra ruthless in making sure that no one has a camera on campus. And he wouldn't have had time to copy it all out by hand."

"So what was he doing?" asked Pauline.

"My guess is he brought his own homework in here and checked it against yours," said Friday. "If he had any errors, he could have quickly made the corrections."

She bent down and picked something up from the floor. "Is this yours?" Friday held up a lead pencil that had been thoroughly chewed on one end.

"Gross! I would never chew a pencil," said Pauline. "Think of all the chemicals in the paint."

"It's not mine either," said Sienna. "I only use mechanical pencils. I had a nasty accident with a pencil sharpener as a small child."

Friday closely inspected the chewed end of the pencil. "From the evidence we have so far, we can conclude that you were tricked into going upstairs by a very tall boy with a crooked left incisor and a nervous temperament, who is good at math but who desperately wants to be better. Does that sound like anyone you know?"

"Well, yes . . . Michael Cathguard," said Pauline.

"He's her math nemesis," explained Sienna.

"For four years we've competed against each other for top position in math," said Pauline. "But over the last six months he's dropped behind. Michael has struggled to grasp some of the fundamental principles of calculus."

"We'll have to talk to him, then," said Friday.

Melanie yawned and opened her eyes. "I just had a

dream about Michael Cathguard. He was standing over me reading a sheet of paper; then a leg came through the ceiling, and he ran away. Dreams are always so silly, aren't they?"

"In this case, it appears reality is even sillier," said Friday. "Let's go knock on his door. We know he's awake."

The girls trooped downstairs for the dramatic confrontation. Friday was just about to knock on Michael's door when they heard a commotion.

"Dette kan ikke fortsette!" yelled a girl.

Friday leaned in close to the door. "That's not Michael."

"It's coming from over there," said Melanie. They all turned and looked at the door on the other side of the corridor.

"That's the bodyguard's room," said Pauline.

"Really? Mr. Rasmus lives here? That's a coincidence," said Friday.

"But who's yelling at him?" asked Melanie.

"Hun er uutholdelig!" yelled the girl.

"She's yelling in Norwegian," said Friday. "It must be Princess Ingrid."

Suddenly the door burst open and Debbie stepped

out, slamming the door behind her. She was wearing a large, bulky dressing gown, which had been buttoned up right to her chin. Debbie was flushed in the face, but her cheeks grew redder when she saw how many people were standing in the corridor.

"I didn't know you speak Norwegian," said Friday.

"I speak Danish," said Debbie. "It's very similar."

"Why were you yelling at Mr. Rasmus?" asked Friday.

"And in the middle of the night?" asked Melanie. "Don't you know how important it is to get a full eight hours of sleep?"

"I can't say," said Debbie. "It's to do with the princess and how she behaves."

"She's being an enormous pain, and you're tired of sharing a room with her, aren't you?" guessed Melanie.

A door opened behind them. They all turned to see Michael Cathguard peering out from the crack. "You know, don't you?" he asked, guiltily.

"Let's discuss this in your room," said Friday, pushing her way in, the other girls following.

Debbie used this opportunity to scurry away.

Michael broke down immediately when Friday confronted him with the facts.

"I admit it. It was me. I'm so sorry," said Michael. "I put the speaker in the attic above your room, and when you marked an 'E' on the beam I made the same mark on every beam to make it harder for you to find the speaker."

"But why?" asked Pauline. "You're still the second-best student at math. Isn't that good enough?"

"My father was so proud when I topped math last

year," explained Michael. "He boasted about it to his friends."

"He must have very boring friends," said Friday.

"He does—he's an accountant," said Michael.

"Anyway, he promised to give me a thousand dollars if I did it again."

"Wow!" said Pauline. "My parents are super ambitious, but they would never do that."

"I don't have to beat you," said Michael. "I'd just have to tie you. I was getting most of the answers right by myself, but there was always one or two that I struggled with. A thousand dollars is a lot of money. I couldn't resist the temptation to cheat."

"Shame on you," said Friday. "What would Pythagoras say?"

"Are you going to tell the Headmaster?" asked Michael.

"That's up to Pauline," said Friday. "She's the client."

"Let me get this straight," said Pauline. "If you get the same grade as me in math and we have a tie, you get a thousand dollars?"

"That's right," said Michael.

"Then let's split the money," said Pauline. "If you promise to share the thousand dollars, I'll go over your homework with you every night and show you how to fix any errors."

"Deal!" exclaimed Michael, putting out his hand.

Pauline shook it.

"I love it when a story ends happily with a mutually beneficial, morally bankrupt collaboration," said Melanie.

21

The Framing of Dr. Barnes

Friday was sitting quietly in history class, secretly reading a book on criminal profiling under the desk. She was trying to work out whether Princess Ingrid was a sociopath or simply had narcissistic personality disorder, when Ian burst through the door.

"Friday, you'd better come quickly!" he said.

"Wainscott! How dare you

interrupt my class," said Mr. Conti. "You'd better have a good reason."

"Sorry, sir," said Ian. "It's just that Friday's father is being arrested, and I thought she'd want to know."

"Okay, that is a good reason," conceded Mr. Conti. "You may go, Friday, and you too, Melanie—I know there's no way you'll stay awake if your friend isn't here."

Friday and Melanie hurried after Ian, who led them across the school at a jog.

"What happened?" asked Friday.

"I was walking past Dr. Barnes's physics classroom when I heard a commotion," said Ian. "I looked in and saw two policemen dragging your father out into the hallway."

"Why did they take him away?" asked Friday.

"I don't know," said Ian. "Look, there's the squad car out in front of the administration building!"

Friday started running faster now. She could see her father and hear him.

"This is an outrage!" yelled Dr. Barnes. "It's the persecution of Galileo all over again."

"We haven't persecuted anyone called Galileo," said

Sergeant Crowley. He ran the local police station and thus had dealt with many strange happenings at the school, which usually involved Friday.

"Dr. Barnes is referring to a sixteenth-century scientist," explained Ian. "Galileo was tormented by the Inquisition and sentenced to house arrest for a decade, for making scientific discoveries that challenged church doctrine."

"He's got a high opinion of himself then, hasn't he?" said Sergeant Crowley. He turned to Dr. Barnes. "Sir, we're not persecuting you for your scientific discoveries. I doubt we could understand even if you explained them to us. We're persecuting you because you've been found to have a large amount of stolen property hidden in your car. You're going to jail for petty theft, not for challenging anyone's fundamental belief system."

"He should get an extra six months for giving me an ulcer," said the Headmaster.

"Headmaster, I'm surprised at you," said Friday. "It has been scientifically proven that stomach ulcers are caused by bacteria, not stress. And besides, if my father has contributed to your stress, you've only got yourself to blame for hiring him."

"You told me to hire him!" protested the Headmaster.

"I'm twelve years old. What are you doing taking advice from me?" asked Friday. "And what's this talk about my father stealing things?!"

"He's the Pimpernel!" said the Vice Principal, a gleam of bloodlust in his eyes. He enjoyed getting people fired. "His car is crammed full of stolen property. He hid the car under a willow tree so the branches would hide his stash, but I saw what he was up to and called the police right away."

"And you let him do this?" Friday demanded of the Headmaster. "You

didn't have to involve
the police."

"My watch was one of
the stolen items in the car," said
the Headmaster.

"But you can't believe that Dad took it
all!" said Friday. "Sergeant Crowley, please, you must see that
my father is far too silly to be
such a competent thief."

"I'm not going to con-
duct an interview with
you standing on the
driveway of a

school," said Sergeant Crowley. "If you'd like to make yourself available for a formal interview, then you may come down to the station."

"But I'm twelve! I can't drive!" argued Friday.

"That's not my problem," said Sergeant Crowley.

"Friday, stay away," urged Dr. Barnes. "The local police are in league with the Nobel Prize Committee. It's a perfect storm of vengeful forces. I think your mother put them up to this."

Sergeant Crowley shut the car door on Dr. Barnes before he could make any more wild allegations.

"I suggest you contact a lawyer," Sergeant Crowley said to Friday. "That's the type of help he needs now." Sergeant Crowley got in the squad car and drove off.

Dr. Barnes turned and yelled something wildly to Friday, but she couldn't hear what he had said through the glass.

"Do you think your father has gone senile?" asked Ian.

"It's definitely a possibility," said Friday.

"I realize I haven't got the firmest grasp on reality," said Melanie, "but that stuff about the local police being in league with the Nobel Prize Committee seemed pretty nutty to me."

"I agree," said Friday. "The Nobel Prize Committee is comprised of some of the finest minds in Europe, so I doubt they'd be seeking out Sergeant Crowley for help."

"Poor Sergeant Crowley. He so dislikes being forced to do work," said Melanie.

"Who do we know who's a lawyer?" asked Friday.

"Half the students at Highcrest have parents who are lawyers," said Melanie. "But I think most of them specialize in the type of law to do with not paying taxes, not the type of law for getting esteemed scientists off theft charges."

"And we don't have any money," said Friday. "So we need a lawyer who owes us a favor."

"I know someone," said Ian.

"You do?" said Friday.

"My mom," said Ian.

Springing Dr. Barnes

Melanie called her father's chauffeur and got him to give them a lift. Friday and Melanie went straight to the police station. Ian arranged for his mother to meet them there, but Ian couldn't go along himself because he had to play in the polo tournament that afternoon. It took Mrs. Wainscott an hour and a half to arrive at the police station, and when she did, Uncle Bernie was with her.

"What are you doing here?" asked Friday.

"I offered to drive Helena," said Uncle Bernie.

"Who?" asked Friday, although had her brain been working with its usual efficiency she should have been able to figure this out.

"Mrs. Wainscott," said Uncle Bernie.

"Why were you with Mrs. Wainscott?" asked Friday.

Uncle Bernie blushed. Blushing is an awkward tell at the best of times. But it is particularly awkward when you are a large, scruffy insurance investigator.

"We were at pottery class when I got your call," said Mrs. Wainscott.

"Pottery class?" said Friday. "Is that code for something else?"

"No, we really do take a pottery class together," said Uncle Bernie.

"Bernard suggested it to me," said Mrs. Wainscott. "I'm always looking for more ways to be self-sufficient. Now I can make my own crockery."

"Hmm," said Friday. "It certainly sounds like a crock to me."

Uncle Bernie blushed again.

"I suppose I'd better meet my client," Mrs. Wainscott said with a giggle. "It's been years since I last did this. This is going to be fun."

Friday rubbed her eyes. "My father is going to jail—I just know it. And the worst part is, I'm going to have to explain all this to my mother."

"You!" snapped Mrs. Wainscott at an officer behind the desk. "I'm Dr. Barnes's legal representative. Show me to him immediately. You better not have been asking him questions before I got here or I'll file a complaint against you for harassment."

"Wow," said Melanie. "Impressive. She must have been a really good acrobat."

"What makes you say that?" asked Friday.

"If she gave up the law to become an acrobat," said Melanie, "she must be even better at twisting herself into a human pretzel than she is at berating police officers."

It was a nervous wait for Friday outside the interview room. She was used to being in the thick of it, not waiting helplessly to find out what was going on.

"What's happening?" asked Friday as Mrs. Wainscott emerged from the interview room, where she had been talking with Sergeant Crowley and Dr. Barnes.

"Your father is acting very strangely," said Mrs. Wainscott. "He keeps muttering about how rival M-theorists are trying to destroy him. Is that some sort of *Star Trek* reference?"

"No, there really are rival M-theorists who would like to destroy him," said Friday. "But you have to understand that in the world of theoretical physics, 'destroying' someone means writing a really well-researched paper disproving their thesis."

"So you're sure he's not seriously mentally ill?" asked Mrs. Wainscott.

"No, all academics act like that," said Friday. "Muttering, irrational thoughts, and obsessive behavior are all socially acceptable in their work environment."

"That's a shame," said Mrs. Wainscott. "If he were bonkers, it would be easier to get him off. If he is sane, he's probably going to get in a lot of trouble. The police found a hundred and eighty thousand dollars' worth of stolen goods in his car."

"What?" exclaimed Friday.

"Apparently it was packed to the roof with stolen computers, jewelry, kitchen appliances, federal bond certificates—"

"Why would anyone have federal bond certificates lying around at school?" asked Friday.

"In case there is a currency crash and they have to

flee the country with easily exchangeable assets," explained Melanie.

"You're kidding," said Friday.

"It happens more than you might expect with the student body at Highcrest," said Melanie. "Last year, the tax department discovered that Hazel Edwards's parents hadn't filed a tax return for fifteen years. They landed their helicopter on the football field, grabbed Hazel, and flew off to the Bahamas to live as tax exiles."

"But my father can't have stolen all those things," said Friday.

"Why? Because he's an essentially honest person?" asked Melanie.

"No, because it would involve carrying heavy objects and packing them into the car," said Friday. "It would be beyond him. He's used to making PhD students do that type of thing for him. PhD students are the academic world's version of indentured slaves. The only reason they get away with it is because the students all have Stockholm syndrome, plus they're under the misapprehension that a PhD is actually worth something."

"But the stolen property was in his car," said

Mrs. Wainscott. "He's paranoid and delusional. That isn't going to look good in court."

"Were his fingerprints on the stolen property?" asked Friday.

"I don't know," said Mrs. Wainscott. "There are so many items, forensics hasn't analyzed them all. But it wouldn't matter. If there were no fingerprints, the police would just argue that he used gloves."

"As if my father would ever do anything that sensible," said Friday.

At that moment Sergeant Crowley emerged from the interview room carrying a plastic tray.

"Are those my father's personal effects?" asked Friday.

"What if they are?" asked Sergeant Crowley.

"I'd like to see them—and the stolen property," said Friday.

"Why on earth would I agree to that?" said Sergeant Crowley.

"Sergeant, there's no use pretending I'm an ordinary twelve-year-old," said Friday. "I've already solved several significant cases for your department. You could obstruct my investigation, but if this is all a misunderstanding, the sooner I reveal what's really going on, the less embarrassing it will be for you."

"My inspector would never go for that," said Sergeant Crowley.

"You'll be getting a lot of close attention from your inspector when it's on the six o'clock news that you arrested a Nobel laureate's husband for theft," said Friday. "That would be fine if your accusations were entirely correct, but if your case is going to collapse, surely it's better if that happens now, before the international news crews set up their cameras in the parking lot."

Sergeant Crowley sighed. He didn't want to agree because, being a police sergeant, he was trained not to be agreeable. But he liked being in charge of a small-town police station, precisely because it was quiet and there wasn't much for him to do. If Friday did solve the case and make the whole thing disappear, he would be secretly relieved.

"All right," he said. "But you'll owe me a favor."

"Agreed," said Friday. "You can call on me any time your own investigative team lets you down."

"*Harrumph*," said Sergeant Crowley. "If I did that, you'd need to have your own office; you'd be here full-time. Come on, I'll show you the evidence room."

Sergeant Crowley led Friday, Melanie, Uncle Bernie, and Mrs. Wainscott to a room at the back of the police station. Then he opened the door and ushered them inside.

There were steel shelves laden with labeled evidence bags. In the middle of the room was a large table where two junior officers were putting items into more evidence bags.

"Everything on the table was found in your father's car," said Sergeant Crowley.

"Wow, that's a lot of stuff," said Melanie. "I can't believe he fit that all in."

"It was very meticulously packed," said Sergeant Crowley. "There wasn't a spare inch of space, other than the driver's seat."

Friday took out her magnifying glass and approached the table.

"You can look, but no touching," said Sergeant Crowley. "I can't have you contaminating the evidence."

"Understood," said Friday as she leaned in to peer at the first bag. It took her forty minutes to fully inspect every object. The process involved a certain amount of crouching down and crawling on the floor as she

struggled to inspect each piece from every angle without touching it.

"Your father certainly has eclectic taste in stolen property," observed Melanie. "The laptop, jewelry, and bond certificates I can understand, but what would he want with a set of carbon-fiber golf clubs? If he's anything like you, he would never be able to hit the ball."

"They're all things he could easily fence for cash," said Sergeant Crowley. "Pawnshops will always take golf clubs and computers."

"Where are my father's personal effects?" asked Friday. "The things you took off him when he arrived?"

"In here." The sergeant placed the small plastic tray on the table in front of Friday.

"Hmm . . . interesting." Friday carefully inspected each item. There was a pair of frayed shoelaces. A wallet. A five-dollar bill and sixty cents in loose change. A notebook covered in scribbled equations and a blunt pencil.

"Tell me," said Friday, "how did you get into the car to take everything out?"

"It was locked," said Sergeant Crowley. "But Constable Benson used to work with auto theft. He can break into any car in less than ten seconds."

"How?" asked Melanie.

"That's privileged information," said Sergeant Crowley.

"He smashed the driver's window," said Friday. "I know because there are tiny fragments of auto glass in with several of the stolen items."

"Yes, well, apparently that's how all the big-city police departments do it these days," said Sergeant Crowley.

"You really should read some of the industry periodicals you have stored out in your waiting room," said Friday. "One of these days someone other than me is going to notice your total lack of knowledge of any investigative technique developed in the twenty years since you left the police academy."

"Hey," said Sergeant Crowley, "I'm doing you a favor letting you see this! There's no reason for you to give me lip."

"Except for the fact that you wrongly arrested my father," said Friday.

"Here we go," said Sergeant Crowley, shaking his head. "I know he's your dad, but I won't stand for any of your nonsense and tricks just so you can get him off the hook."

"I don't need nonsense or tricks," said Friday. "The evidence speaks for itself."

"What are you talking about?" demanded Sergeant Crowley.

"There is no way my father could have packed all this property into one Ford Cortina," said Friday. "He hasn't got the patience, spatial awareness, or hand-eye coordination for such a complicated task."

"But he's a genius," said Sergeant Crowley. "He could figure it out."

"You clearly don't know many geniuses," said Friday. "I, on the other hand, grew up in a house with six geniuses, aside from myself."

"Thanks for the touch of modesty," said Sergeant Crowley, rolling his eyes.

"I'm only being truthful," said Friday. "Anyway, the thing about geniuses is that they find some things so utterly easy, such as understanding the space-time continuum, that they come to resent anything that is not equally easy, such as deciding what to wear in the morning, or packing a car. Because it doesn't come as simply to them, they dismiss it as trivial and make no attempt. There is no way my father would have attempted packing all these objects into a car.

To him, it would be equivalent to building castles in a sandpit."

"I like building sandcastles," said Melanie.

"Yes, but you'd have the good sense to do it wearing a swimsuit," said Friday. "Father would try it wearing a tweed jacket and loafers, then give up because he was uncomfortable."

"That isn't even circumstantial evidence," said Sergeant Crowley. "It's just speculation and hypothesis."

"Then there's the fact that my father has never in his life done anything for the money," continued Friday. "We never had spare cash. When my school had an overnight field trip to the national science museum, I had to wash all the neighbors' cars to pay for myself to go."

"Again, that's just conjecture," said Sergeant Crowley.

"No, it's not," said Friday. "Why would he steal a carload of property? If he wanted money, he could just take a job with one of the many defense contractors who are constantly wooing him to design the next generation of missiles."

Sergeant Crowley was astonished. "That blithering loony in there has been headhunted to design military-grade weapons?!"

"I know. It's horrifying, isn't it?" said Friday.

"Perhaps he did all this because he's finally gone bananas," said Sergeant Crowley. "Your mother went off to Europe without him. Perhaps that tipped him over the edge and all this is a cry for help?"

"I like that idea," said Mrs. Wainscott. "I can use that in court."

"Perhaps," said Friday. "But if so, answer me this— how did he get it all in the car?"

"What do you mean?" asked Sergeant Crowley. "Through the door."

"But *how*?" said Friday. "You have all his personal possessions right here and, as you can see, there is no key. No keys at all. When you found the car it was locked."

"What are you saying?" asked Sergeant Crowley.

"The person who stole this property," said Friday, "is the person who has Dad's keys. No doubt he or she stole them."

"The Pimpernel," said Melanie.

"But surely your father would notice if someone stole his keys?" said Sergeant Crowley.

"He wouldn't notice if you tied him to train tracks in front of an oncoming train," said Friday.

"But he'd notice when he tried to drive the car," said Sergeant Crowley.

"But he hasn't tried to drive the car," said Friday. "The engine doesn't work. The football team had to push it into that parking space."

"I can't release him just on the basis that his car keys are missing," said Sergeant Crowley.

"Before you formally charge him in front of a judge," said Friday, "I suggest you make a concerted effort to find those keys. This could be embarrassing for you. While my mother is in Europe now, it would only take a day for her to get here, with my brothers and sisters. And the only thing worse than dealing with one doctor of theoretical physics is trying to reason with six of them."

"I'll get on it," said Sergeant Crowley.

"As will I," said Friday. "No one frames my father for a crime he didn't commit, no matter how irritating he is. Something sneaky is going on at Highcrest Academy, and I'm going to get to the bottom of it."

The Pretender

When Friday and Melanie got back to Highcrest
Academy it was a hive of activity. A marquee had been
set up alongside the polo field, and an announcer's
voice could be heard on the wind
describing the pedigrees of vari-
ous polo ponies.

"The polo tournament must
be about to start," said Friday.

"That's going to make it
hard for you to investigate
the accusations against
your father," said Mel-
anie.

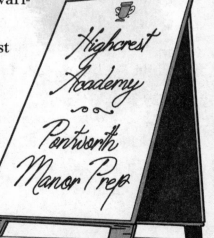

"Not at all," said Friday. "It will make it easy because all the suspects are in one place."

"So who are your suspects?" asked Melanie.

"It depends on the motive," said Friday. "If it was to get my father fired, then it could be anyone on the science staff he has humiliated with his superior knowledge and grating lack of social skills."

"Which is everyone on the science staff," said Melanie.

"Exactly," agreed Friday. "But the motive could be simpler. It could be about money. Someone stole the goods to sell for money. And the unusable car was a convenient place to hide them. So it would be someone who needs or really, really wants lots of money."

"None of the students here really need any more money," said Melanie.

"Except for Ian," said Friday. "It's going to take a while for his mother to sort out her financial difficulties."

"It could be a member of the staff," said Melanie. "Teachers aren't paid well."

"The teachers here are," said Friday. "They have to be to put up with the obnoxious students. But I agree the teachers are more in need of spare cash than the students."

"And the Headmaster does have a gambling problem," added Melanie.

"Good point," said Friday.

"It could be someone who liked stealing things for the thrill of it," said Melanie. "Perhaps because they've seen too many reruns of *Robin Hood*, which I've always thought over-glamorized theft."

"Really, when it comes down to it, it could be anybody in the entire school," said Friday. "Even people who don't need the money might do it out of petty spite because they've lived such privileged lives they have an almost sociopathic disregard for the suffering of others."

"We can't search the whole school," said Melanie.

"No," said Friday. "Which means we will need to set a trap."

"You mean like a wire cage that you use to capture a possum in the attic?" asked Melanie.

"I don't think you can buy wire cages in human sizes," said Friday. "We'll just have to set some bait and lure the thief out."

"But how will you actually capture them?" asked Melanie.

"I'll worry about that bit later," said Friday. "Let's go check out this polo match."

There was a carnival atmosphere down on the polo field. Parents carrying glasses of champagne laughed too loudly at each other's jokes, while students lounged about, as far away from the adults as possible, enjoying an afternoon off in the sun when they would normally be inside ignoring some tedious lesson. Parker, an eighth-grade boy, was at the microphone making all the public address announcements.

"Why on earth did they let Parker do the announcements?" asked Friday. "He's not terribly verbose at the best of times."

"I think that's the reason," said Melanie. "They let the Vice Principal do it last year, and he was such a windbag he drove everyone to despair. The Headmaster wanted someone who could be trusted to use absolutely no initiative and only say exactly what he had been told to say."

"I see," said Friday. "We can use that to our advantage."

"By 'our advantage,' you mean 'your advantage,'

don't you?" said Melanie. "Because I've got absolutely no idea what you're talking about."

"Naturally." Friday took a notebook and pencil out of her pocket. "I'm going to write a script for Parker." She started busily scribbling away.

"Make sure you don't use cursive," said Melanie. "He can't read that."

A few minutes later, Friday was approaching Parker in the announcer's tent with her script in hand. Mrs. Cannon, their English teacher, was sitting next to Parker as he read through the list of players.

"Today Ian Wainscott will be riding Valiant Fury, Valkyrie, and Butterfly Buttons," read Parker.

"Mrs. Cannon is obviously there to keep an eye on Parker," said Friday. "To make sure he doesn't lose his head and say something outrageous."

"It sounds like the perfect job for her," said Melanie. "There's no way that could happen, so she can just have a little nap if she likes."

"Well, you're going to have to distract her," said Friday. "Because saying something shocking and untrue is exactly what I want Parker to do."

"All right," said Melanie.

The girls walked up to the desk. "Hello, Mrs. Cannon," said Melanie. "Friday wants me to distract you so that she can get Parker to say something that isn't on his official script."

"Really?" said Mrs. Cannon. "That sounds intriguing. Much more intriguing than this unspeakably boring polo match. Why don't you pretend to sprain your ankle—then I could pretend to be concerned."

"Okay," said Melanie. "Does that mean I can lie down?"

"I wouldn't dream of trying to stop you," said Mrs. Cannon. "I just wish I could do the same."

"You could say you had a fainting spell," suggested Melanie.

"What a good idea," said Mrs. Cannon. "If you've got a sprained ankle and I have a fainting spell, then we can both have a nice rest on the grass."

"The Headmaster can't complain about that," said Melanie as they both made themselves comfortable.

"Of course not," said Mrs. Cannon. "If he did I'd report him to my union."

"Parker, I need you to read this," said Friday, handing him her handwritten script.

"Will I get in trouble?" asked Parker.

"If everything goes to plan, no one will think to be mad at you because they'll all be far angrier with someone else," said Friday.

"Okay," said Parker. "That's all right, then . . . Let's have a look." Parker picked up the paper and started reading. "Ladies and gentlemen, I will now describe the Trumpley Cup for you. It was handmade eighty years ago by Spanish craftsmen using solid gold. Aside from its incalculable value as an antique and part of our school's cultural history, if it were melted down the gold alone would be worth one hundred thousand dollars."

The crowd gasped. They were all gathered along the sideline near the announcer's tent, and they turned around to look at the Trumpley Cup, which until that point had been ignored as another boring sporting trophy. The cup glistened in the sunlight. It was unmistakably golden, but people had naturally assumed it was gold-plated. Here, in the heady atmosphere of a polo tournament surrounded by ridiculously rich students and parents, the idea that it was made of solid gold seemed entirely probable.

Friday scanned the crowd to see if anyone was behaving suspiciously. Several people were staring at the cup with open lust. A couple of parents had even taken out their smartphones to do a few calculations on the value, and how much they could earn if they invested the money in an illegal offshore tax avoidance scheme.

"Is that all you needed me to do?" asked Parker.

"For now, yes. Thank you, Parker," said Friday. "We've set the trap. Now we just have to wait for someone to take the bait. Come on, Melanie, wake up. We've got to watch the match."

"Can we stand by the pony lines?" asked Melanie, yawning. "I like ponies. They're like unicorns with lower aspirations."

"I'd better get the match started, then, I suppose." Parker leaned into the microphone. "Teams, take your positions. We are ready to start play."

Chapter
24
The Match

The teams trotted into position on opposing sides of the field. The umpire held up the ball, and everyone was silent for a moment; then he tossed it onto the field. What followed was a frenzy of whacking mallets, whinnying horses, and teenagers swearing at each other like sailors. Although there really was no need to use such colorful language when essentially all they were saying was "Get out of the way."

Soon Ian managed to flick the ball out into open field and took off galloping after it. The opposition wheeled around to give chase, but Ian was already several lengths ahead and traveling at full speed. He only had one horseman to get past. The defender was thundering down the field to intercept him.

"Oh my gosh," said Friday. "I hope Ian's going to be all right. That's an awfully big horse."

"Did you hear that, ladies and gentlemen?" said Parker into the microphone. "Ian Wainscott's girl-friend is seriously concerned for his safety."

"Parker!" exclaimed Friday. "Don't announce that to the whole school."

"You're standing so close to the microphone that they all heard you say it," said Parker.

"They're going to collide!" exclaimed Friday.

Ian and the opposing defender were powering toward each other in a direct line. Ian was obviously banking that his opponent would flinch first and pull out of the collision, but from where Friday was standing she had a better view of the boy's face. He didn't look intelligent enough to do something so sensible.

Just at the last moment, Ian deftly flicked his mallet and hit the ball across the field to Princess Ingrid, who, unnoticed by anyone, was galloping up the opposite wing. Ian slammed into the defender in a sickening collision. Luckily, the defender was leaning out of his saddle, so he took most of the weight of the blow and the horses were unharmed. Ian fell out of his saddle, landing on his bottom. He looked up just in time to see Princess Ingrid smack the ball into the goal.

"GOAL!" roared Parker.

Ian picked himself up and was apparently unhurt, because he was able to jog over to the lines and get up onto another pony.

"I had previously thought all sports were stupid," said Friday, "but witnessing this—a game played with horses and big, long mallets—I realize that sports are capable of a whole greater level of idiocy than I had ever imagined."

And so the game progressed. Highcrest Academy and Pontworth Manor Prep were well matched. Pontworth Prep had a lean Argentinean player called José—who had superb strength, amazing agility, and absolutely zero scruples about cheating—as well as two brutes who seemed larger than the ponies they were riding, and a solidly built Irish girl who could scare the ponies with the vehemence of her swearing.

But Highcrest had a strong lineup, too. Ian's marvelous balance in the saddle, Binky's dogged determination, Nigel's total disregard for his own safety, and Princess Ingrid's superior horsemanship gave their team a good chance. By the end of the third quarter, Highcrest Academy was only one point behind.

Friday watched Ian trot back to the lines. He was tired and drenched in sweat. He looked down and caught her eye.

"Are you all right?" asked Friday.

"What's this?" said Ian. "The great detective showing human empathy. Perhaps the rumors that you're a cyborg aren't true after all."

"That horse hit your leg very hard," said Friday.

"Can it," said Ian as he got down to change ponies. "I don't need your sympathy."

"I don't suppose you do," said Friday. "You need an ice pack. Crush injuries should be treated with ice and elevation."

"Is that what the database that you have instead of a brain tells you?" asked Ian.

"I'm sure Mrs. Marigold will lend you a packet of frozen peas if you need them," said Friday.

"Thanks for the advice," said Ian.

"Well played, Wainscott," said the Vice Principal. "You, too, Your Highness." He bowed to Princess Ingrid. "In the next chukka I want you to concentrate on zone defense. You're only one point behind—hold on to that, and then attack in the last five minutes when they're tired."

"We're already tired," said Ian.

"I'm the coach, and I say that's the strategy you should use," said the Vice Principal.

"You are not qualified to spit on my boots, let alone tell me how to play polo," said Princess Ingrid as she swung up into her saddle. "I play not just to win, but to destroy my enemy."

"You mean opposition," said Binky.

"They are my enemies," said Princess Ingrid. "Most of you are, too, so watch it." She kicked her horse and cantered back toward the field.

"The strategy I'm going to use is getting the ball into the goal," said Ian. "I hope that works for everyone, because I'm too pooped for anything more complicated."

As the match resumed, Pontworth Manor Prep had obviously made a team decision to elevate their poor sportsmanship to a higher level. As José passed

Princess Ingrid with the ball, he pretended to swing at the ball but then whacked her pony hard in the ribs with his mallet. Princess Ingrid's pony reared, whinnying as José galloped down the field to score in the undefended goal.

"It would be one thing if he'd hit Princess Ingrid with a mallet," said Melanie angrily, "but to hit her pony is just cruel."

"Ian looks angry," said Friday.

"You can't tear your eyes away from him for a moment, can you?" said Melanie.

"Look," said Friday.

Ian had the ball and was taking it up the wing.

José was steaming across the field to intercept him. "Ian's going to be squashed," said Friday.

"You should have more faith in him," said Melanie.

"It's got nothing to do with faith," said Friday. "It's all about physics. José has more momentum."

They were just about to crash into each other, when Ian whacked the ball with a deft backward flick, passing it to Binky. José pulled up his horse, looking over his shoulder and trying to wheel around. But José's pony had had enough of her belligerent rider. She dug in her front hooves, lowered her head, and threw José onto the ground right at Friday's feet. José lay flat on his back gasping for air.

"Serves you right, you nasty animal basher," said Ian.

"Poor sportsmanship!" wailed the Pontworth Prep coach. "He did that on purpose."

"Ian didn't do anything," said Melanie. "It was the pony who did it on purpose."

The Vice Principal rushed forward to help the Pontworth Prep coach get José to his feet. The other players trotted over.

"He's fine," said the Vice Principal. "Just winded. You'll be able to keep playing, won't you, son?"

José nodded. *"Sí, sí."*

As the Vice Principal let him go, Friday noticed a mark on José's upper arm. "Is that a smallpox vaccination scar?" she asked.

"Of course, so what?" said José as he dusted horse muck from the seat of his trousers.

"Barnes! It's not good manners to draw attention to our visitor's scar," snapped the Vice Principal.

"I didn't point it out to be rude," said Friday. "I pointed it out to accuse him of cheating."

"What?!" exploded the Vice Principal.

"This is an outrage!" declared Pontworth Prep's polo coach. "How dare my player be insulted in the middle of a match! This is all just a ploy to psych him out, isn't it?"

"No," said Friday. "I couldn't care less who wins the match."

"What about school pride?" demanded the Vice Principal.

"I don't think the school should be proud of the results of four of their students riding around on horses whacking a ball," said Friday.

"They're called ponies," said Melanie.

"Which I totally don't understand," said Friday. "The vast majority of them are over fourteen hands high at the withers, which is the distinction between a pony and a horse."

"It's traditional to call them ponies," said Ian.

"It's irrational," said Friday.

"Are you going to make this girl apologize?" demanded the Pontworth Prep polo coach to the Vice Principal. "Or will I have to write an official letter of complaint to your headmaster and the International High School Polo Association?"

"I'm not going to apologize. He confirmed that it is

a smallpox vaccination scar, and the World Health Organization certified smallpox as being eradicated in 1979, which means that José can't be a high school student," said Friday. "He must be well over thirty."

"Perhaps he got held back for poor academic results?" said Melanie.

"No school holds a student back that long," said Friday.

"Thank goodness," said Binky. "Otherwise I'd be here into my fifties."

"José, I'm appalled that you would deceive the school about your true age," said the coach.

"Can it, Roger," said the Vice Principal. "No one believes this crackpot scheme wasn't your idea. You tried using a rodeo bronco last year, and a racing Thoroughbred the year before that. You're always coming up with new and stupid ways to cheat. Tonight there will be an angry letter written to the International High School Polo Association, but it's going to be about you."

"Sirs," interrupted Ian, "this is all very shocking and a terrible blight on the game, but can we just get on with the match? We've got a good chance of winning anyway, even with José being a flagrant cheat. Let's finish the game and have some fun."

The crowd cheered. The riders remounted. Except for José. He was replaced by Pontworth Prep's substitute player, a pimply, lanky, gangly boy.

"That one's definitely a teenager," said Friday.

"Either that or he's suffering a terrible vitamin deficiency," said Melanie.

Play resumed, and Pontworth Prep had clearly lost their mojo. Princess Ingrid could smell blood—she showed no mercy. With Binky setting her up and Ian running interference for her, she was easily able to slam home three more goals, much to the delight of the roaring crowd. When the final siren sounded, the Highcrest students ran onto the field cheering. They stood back while the sweaty horses were led to their grooms. Then they rushed forward again to pick up the four players and carry them on their shoulders to the podium, where the Vice Principal was standing with the Trumpley Cup.

Ian, Princess Ingrid, Nigel, and Binky climbed up on the stage. The Vice Principal leaned in to give his speech. Friday and Melanie wiggled their way to the front of the crowd.

"Here we go," said Friday. "I bet this takes a while."

But it didn't, because at that moment the Vice Principal was interrupted.

"Excuse me, Vice Principal," said the Headmaster, moving between him and the microphone. "I'm sorry to interrupt." The Headmaster reached out and took the cup from the Vice Principal's hands. The Vice Principal looked like he wanted to cry.

"Ladies and gentlemen," said the Headmaster, "we are honored to have a very special guest pay a visit to us today. It is only fitting that we ask him to present this trophy, given that his daughter is part of the victorious team."

Princess Ingrid went from looking triumphant to ghostly pale.

"Please make welcome His Royal Highness—the King of Norway!" The Headmaster stood back and a very elegant but slightly overweight man in a perfectly cut navy-blue suit stepped forward.

"Your Majesty," continued the Headmaster, handing the trophy to him, "if you will be so kind. The Trumpley Cup has been won by your daughter and her team."

The king took the trophy, beamed proudly, and turned to face the victors. Then his face fell. *"Hva pokker er det som skjer?"* he demanded.

No one knew what this meant, but from his tone of voice he was clearly very angry.

"I'm sorry, sir, is there a problem?" asked the Headmaster.

"Who is this?" demanded the king. "She is not my daughter. Where is my daughter? What have you done with her?"

Chapter

25

The King's Daughter

"What?! Nothing! But she told me she was the princess!" protested the Headmaster.

"Your Majesty," said Friday, stepping forward so that she was right in front of the podium. "I think I can help."

The Headmaster dabbed his forehead with a handkerchief. "Please do. Losing a royal princess is not going to look good on my résumé. And I'll need a good résumé because I'll almost certainly be fired if I've lost a royal princess."

"The real Princess Ingrid is perfectly safe and holding Binky's hand," said Friday.

Everyone looked around at Binky. He was standing next to Debbie, holding her hand.

"I'm here, Papa," said Debbie.

"Ingrid!" The king rushed forward to crush her in a hug.

"Ingrid?" exclaimed Binky. "Oh no, I'm totally confused."

"It's true," said Debbie, which was difficult because her father was hugging her so hard he was crushing her chest. "I'm sorry to deceive you, but I am the real Princess Ingrid of Norway."

"I think I'm going to faint," said Binky, looking stunned.

"How did you know?" the princess asked Friday. "I've worked so hard to keep my identity a secret."

"That's why I didn't say anything earlier. I may listen through walls, but I have some respect for the notion of privacy," said Friday. "I realized that the princess wasn't a real princess when she first arrived and my father's car exploded."

"You did?" asked Debbie.

"Mr. Rasmus didn't rush to her," said Friday. "He rushed at Ian. We thought he suspected Ian of being responsible. But Ian was standing in front of you. Mr. Rasmus rushed to knock you down to protect you from danger. Once I suspected that Ingrid wasn't the real princess, there were lots more clues. There was your hostility toward the princess. The plain lenses in your glasses—which Melanie noticed. And most significantly, there was Ingrid's distaste for fish. With Norway's long coastline and proud fishing heritage, there is no way a Norwegian princess would ever denounce the taste of fish. And finally there was the time you yelled at Mr. Rasmus in Norwegian in the middle of the night."

"I suppose that was pretty suspicious," admitted Debbie. "I'm sorry. I hired an actress to pretend to be me so that for the first time in my life I could really be . . . me." She turned to Binky. "I hope you can forgive me. I just wanted to experience middle school as a normal student."

"Oh yes, I'll forgive you," said Binky. "No need to worry about that. You'll just have to wait until the blood stops rushing in my ears and I stop hyperventilating."

"But no normal student would ever want to go to middle school," said Melanie. "Not if she could lounge around a European castle instead."

"Mr. Rasmus," said the King of Norway, turning on the bodyguard, who was standing at the back of the stage. "Did you support this debacle?"

"Yes, Your Highness," said Mr. Rasmus, staring at his shoes.

"Your job is to take care of the princess, the *real* princess!" yelled the King of Norway.

"I thought she would be safer with a decoy," said Mr. Rasmus. "And she left me no choice. Your daughter can be very forceful when she wants to be."

"You can?" asked Binky.

"My time here at Highcrest has been the happiest of my life," said Debbie.

"Really?" said the Headmaster, who was pleased but secretly suspicious he must be doing something wrong if a child was enjoying school that much.

"Sorry to interrupt," said Melanie, "but why is Princess Ingrid the impostor galloping away on her pony?"

Princess Ingrid was indeed galloping at full speed across the polo field, heading toward the swamp. She had something bright and shiny tucked under her arm.

"She's stolen the cup!" said Friday. "She's the Pimpernel!"

Friday instinctively started running after her, although goodness knew why. She never could have caught Princess Ingrid if she were chasing her on foot, but to chase the princess when she was galloping away on horseback was positively ridiculous.

Then suddenly Friday found herself grabbed under her arms and hoisted upward. Ian had pulled her onto the back of his pony. "Hang on tight," he warned. Ian urged his mount forward, and they took off in pursuit. Friday clung to Ian like a barnacle to a rock. Her cheek was pressed against his shoulder blade, and her arms were wrapped tightly around his disgustingly sweaty polo shirt. The pony was throwing up great clods of dirt behind them as they powered across the field and lunged into the swamp, following the sound of Princess Ingrid's hoofbeats.

"She's heading for Mr. Pilcher's motorboat," said Friday.

"Duck," said Ian.

"You think she's heading for a duck?" asked Friday.

"No, *duck*!" said Ian.

Friday looked up to see a low-hanging branch inches from her face. She ducked.

"There! Up ahead," said Ian.

In front of them Princess Ingrid had dismounted and

was climbing into the boat. She turned the engine on and started guiding the boat out into open water.

"We've got to stop her!" yelled Ian.

"No, just let her go," said Friday.

"No way," said Ian. "She's got the cup." He urged his pony into the water.

"Stop!" said Friday. "It's just a cup!"

"That's worth a hundred thousand dollars!" said Ian.

At that moment the decision was made for them, because it turned out that Ian's pony did not care to take a bath. When Butterfly Buttons found herself shin-deep in mud and water, she decided she'd had enough, reared, and threw Friday and Ian off before cantering back to her nice warm stable at the school.

Friday and Ian landed ingloriously in the thick, stinky swamp mud.

"Fantastic," said Ian. "We're covered in mud, the school lost a hundred-thousand-dollar trophy, and Princess Ingrid has gotten away."

"Only one of those three facts is correct," said Friday.

"What are you talking about?" Ian struggled to stand as the viscous mud fought his efforts.

"The cup is not worth a hundred thousand dollars," said Friday. "I made Parker say that to draw out the thief. It's really just gold-plated. It cost the school eighteen dollars to have it made back in 1938."

"Which other fact is incorrect?" asked Ian.

"Princess Ingrid has not gotten away," said Friday, pointing to the boat.

Ian turned to see the boat slowly cruise to a halt. "I siphoned most of the petrol out last night," said Friday. "I wasn't sure who the Pimpernel was, but I didn't want to leave an escape route open before I found out."

"What if she makes a swim for it?" asked Ian.

"I doubt she will," said Friday. "Most northern Europeans are only moderately good at swimming. Besides, she's phobic of fish. So she'd never even dip her toe in the water."

They could hear a siren in the distance. "What's that?" asked Ian.

"While you were playing polo, I borrowed Mrs.

Cannon's phone to alert the coast guard that an act of smuggling would be taking place here, at precisely this time," said Friday, checking her watch. "They're actually a couple of minutes late. I'll have to have a word with their chief about that."

Chapter
26
The Truth Revealed

Later that afternoon Friday sat on the platform alongside the polo field reviewing the day's events with the Headmaster, Ian, Debbie, Melanie, and Dr. Barnes. Friday's father had been released when Princess Ingrid, whose real name was Karin Jonas, had confessed to the entire litany of theft that had taken place at the school over the previous six weeks. Dr. Barnes sat with his head in his hands, not saying very much. He was still extremely confused.

The Headmaster was pretty flustered as well. "So I have been bending over backward to accommodate every whim of some unknown Norwegian child actress?" he asked.

"She's actually very well-known in Norway," said Debbie. "She's a soap opera actress. In hindsight, I suppose I should have taken that as a warning sign. Actors are so morally bankrupt."

"But why didn't anybody notice when that photo was in the magazine?" asked Binky, turning to Debbie. "You don't look anything like that other Ingrid. Surely someone Norwegian would have been able to tell."

"Actually," said Debbie, "I do look a lot like that other Ingrid. This isn't my natural hair color, and I'm wearing brown contacts. I'm really blond with blue eyes."

"No way!" exclaimed Binky.

"Are you angry?" asked Debbie.

"I'm very, very confused," said Binky.

"But he usually is," said Melanie.

"I hate to sound superficial," said Binky. "It's just that . . . I fell for a short, dowdy brunette in an ugly blue cardigan."

"I'm still short," said Debbie. "And my cardigan is still ugly."

"True," said Binky. "I know I shouldn't be shallow. It's unchivalrous. I'm sure I can overcome it."

Debbie gave Binky an affectionate squeeze. And he

distractedly kissed the top of her head. He was still very muddled.

"Why don't you have a Norwegian accent?" asked Melanie.

"It can be surprisingly dull living in a castle. There are so many priceless historical artifacts that you can't ever touch," explained Debbie. "So I tend to spend a lot of time watching English-language TV."

"Me too!" said Binky, brightening up. "That's good. We do have things in common."

"But I don't understand why Karin Jonas wanted to steal all those things," said Ian.

"She's an addict," said Debbie. "She's addicted to shoe shopping. I didn't know that when I hired her. But when we were sharing a room I soon realized she was unbalanced. She was driven by an irrational desire to own more and more shoes. She stole all those things so that she could sell them and buy even more shoes. My father will arrange for her to be sent home to Norway and get treatment there."

"How long have you known she was the Pimpernel?" asked Friday.

"I didn't know for sure, but I suspected," said

Debbie. "I have been looking for her stash, hoping that I could return the stolen property. It was clever of her to hide it all in your father's broken-down car. I never thought of looking there."

"So how long have *you* known?" Ian asked Friday.

"Since you told me," said Friday.

"Me?!" said Ian. "What do you mean?"

"When her necklace got caught on your shirt," said Friday. "You said she had a pair of diamond-encrusted scissors in her pocket that were so sharp they easily sliced through your heavy cotton shirt. That's how she sliced off the Headmaster's watch and your lanyard. But it was only a suspicion. I needed proof before I could say anything."

"I see," said Ian.

"And of course you did your best to put me off the right track," said Friday.

Ian smiled.

"He did?" asked Melanie.

"Karin Jonas may be the thief," said Friday, "but I suspect that Ian is the elusive Aquamarine Pimpernel."

"You can't prove that," said Ian.

"No," agreed Friday, "but if the calling cards weren't left lying around by the thief, they must have been made up as a joke by someone with a devious sense of humor. Someone who enjoys creating a stir."

"That does sound like Ian," said Melanie.

"I can't believe it," said the Headmaster. "The Pimpernel is just a joke. And you"—he turned to Debbie—"a girl I've hardly noticed, are in fact heir to the throne of Norway!"

"Yes, I'm afraid so," said Debbie. "I wear these thick glasses and drab clothes so that the paparazzi won't want to take my picture."

"I think your thick glasses and drab clothes are beautiful," said Binky.

Debbie smiled. "That's what I like about you. Your simplicity."

"And the Haakon Stone is safe," said the Headmaster, taking the pink diamond necklace from his pocket. "We were able to get it back from the fake princess before the police took her away. I am pleased to be able to return it to you, Your Highness." He handed the necklace to Debbie.

"Oh, that isn't the Haakon Stone," said Debbie.

"It's not?" asked Friday.

"No, it's just a diamond," said Debbie, putting it in her pocket. "I lent it to Karin so that she would look the part of a European princess."

"Just a diamond!" exclaimed Ian. "A diamond that size must be worth a fortune."

"I suppose so," said Debbie. "But this is the real Haakon Stone." She pulled the leather strap out from around her neck and showed them the pebble she always wore. "It's an ancient symbol of the Norwegian royal family, so it's much more valuable."

"And you've been wearing it next to your room key all this time?" asked Friday.

"It was a very handy tip," said Debbie. "I haven't locked myself out of my room since."

A rumbling motor sounded in the distance. Melanie shaded her eyes as she looked up into the sky. "Is that a helicopter?"

"No one has asked for permission to land a helicopter here," said the Headmaster. "I do hope it's not one of the parents grabbing their children before they run off to a tax haven. They never pay their school fees when they do."

"It's louder than a normal helicopter," said Ian. "It sounds military."

The pale-blue helicopter was descending toward the polo field.

"Am I the only princess enrolled here?" asked Debbie.

"I think so," said the Headmaster. "Although I wouldn't rule anything out after today."

"Why do you ask?" asked Friday.

"Because that is a Swedish military helicopter," said Debbie.

"I don't know anyone from Sweden," said the Headmaster.

"Oh dear," said Friday. "I do."

The helicopter landed, the pilot cut the engine, and the door swung open. A dowdy middle-aged woman, wearing a brown cardigan and with terribly untidy hair, stepped out.

"Who is it?" asked the Headmaster. "She looks like a scarecrow."

"Evangeline!" exclaimed Dr. Barnes.

"Who?" asked the Headmaster.

"My mother," said Friday.

"The *other* Dr. Barnes," said Ian.

"Actually, if you include my brothers and sisters," said Friday, "she is one of six Barnes doctors. It gets very confusing."

Friday's father started running toward his wife. "Does your family get some sort of bulk discount from an ugly brown cardigan shop?" asked Melanie.

Friday's mother jogged toward her husband, her arms flung wide ready to embrace him. She wasn't very good at running. There was a lot of wobbling and not a lot of forward movement.

"This would be like a scene from a romance movie if they both weren't so wildly uncoordinated," said Melanie.

Friday's mother tripped over a clump of grass, and Friday's father stumbled over his own shoelaces. They collapsed on top of each other on the grass.

"Oh, Rupert," said Friday's mother.

Ian snorted a laugh. "Your father's name is Rupert."

"On the list of embarrassing facts about my father, that doesn't even make the top one thousand," said Friday.

"You came back for me," said Friday's father.

"I need you," said Friday's mother.

"You realized you need me to help analyze your equations?" said Friday's father.

"Yes, I suppose I did," said Friday's mother. "Also, I can't bear traveling without you. Hotel rooms are horrible. I can never get the lid off the jar of macadamias myself."

"Oh, Evangeline," said Friday's father. "How I've longed to hear you say that."

"He's longed for her to want help opening a jar?" asked Ian.

"You've got to understand that neither of them is listening to the other," explained Friday. "It's like a chimpanzee communicating with a gorilla. They're making noises, but the communication is essentially nonverbal."

Both of Friday's parents turned to the helicopter,

and walked toward it arm in arm. The pilot turned the engine back on, and the blades started whipping around again.

Friday stood up and took a step forward. "They're not going back to Sweden without saying goodbye, are they?" she asked.

Her parents climbed into the helicopter and shut the door behind them, without even a backward glance.

"I think they are," said Melanie in response.

"I just got Dad off multiple theft charges," said Friday, "and Mom didn't even say hello, let alone goodbye. I thought I was jaded to my parents' insensitive ways, but this . . . this . . ." She swallowed. She did not want to cry. "This is a new low."

No one said anything. No one knew what to say. Ian took a step forward and put his arm around Friday's shoulders. "Just think—if you didn't have inept parents, you wouldn't be who you are today."

Friday looked up. Ian was looking at her with a sad smile. She realized the same was true for him.

"Would you like us to step away so you can have your first kiss?" asked Melanie. "Unless you've already had your first kiss and I missed it, perhaps because I was napping."

Friday groaned. Ian dropped his arm. The moment was over.

"Come along," said the Headmaster. "Mrs. Marigold's making pepperoni pizza for dinner. She might even hand out seconds of dessert when she finds out your father has gone."

But Friday never got to find out. When she got to the dining room Uncle Bernie was there waiting for her, and with him were two people, a man and a woman wearing dark gray suits and sunglasses.

"Who are they?" asked the Headmaster.

"The big scruffy man in the creased suit is my uncle Bernie," said Friday.

"Perhaps soon to be Ian's stepdad," added Melanie.

"He is not!" said Ian.

"And the other two," said Friday, "given their suits with a high polyester content and ostentatious wearing of sunglasses, I deduce are some sort of government officials."

"Friday!" exclaimed Uncle Bernie as soon as he saw her. "I'm so sorry. There was nothing I could do."

"About what?" asked Friday.

The woman pulled an identification card from her pocket and introduced herself. "I'm Agent Torres from the Department of Immigration. You'll have to come with us."

"Why?" asked Friday.

"You're being deported," said Uncle Bernie.

"On what grounds?" asked the Headmaster. "She hasn't committed a crime. Not one that's been proven, anyway."

"We're deporting her because she's not a citizen," said Agent Torres.

"Yes, I am," said Friday.

"Is it true you were born in Switzerland?" asked Agent Torres.

"Well, yes," conceded Friday.

"Not only that, she's not Friday Barnes," said Agent Torres.

To be continued . . .

Is Friday really not a citizen?

Will she be deported and sent away?

Will Ian Wainscott ever get around
to kissing her?

Find out in book 4,

A Friday Barnes Mystery

NO RULES

COMING SUMMER 2017!